Two Weeks and a Day

Finn's Pub Romance
Book 2

R.G. ALEXANDER

Two Weeks and a Day

Edited by D.S. Editing
Formatted by IRONHORSE Formatting

ISBN: 172727217X
ISBN-13: 978-1727272178

Dedication

To Cookie--Love is the reason
Thank you Robin, for always being there.
Finn Club Forever
And honorable mention to
Nicholas Cage and Roberta Flack.
You'll get it later.

CHAPTER ONE

Cupid Fail

Miller

A *thirty-year-old virgin sits in a crowded pub, fondling his nuts...*

Yeah, don't get your hopes up—this isn't the start of a porno. As usual when it comes to my social life, it isn't as exciting as it sounds.

Why did I agree to this again?

"Earth to Miller Day."

Glancing up from the bowl of bar nuts I've been absently sorting through, I freeze like a damn squirrel catching sight of a predator. There's the look I've been dreading all night—Austen Wayne is on to me.

Desperate to delay the inevitable, I say the first thing that pops into my head. "I was just thinking about turning over a new leaf. Going out more, you know? I could see myself being a regular at a place like this. A pub guy. Maybe I'd hang out with those three old men holding down the bar. Though from where I'm sitting now, I've got the perfect view of a group of off-duty fireman playing darts."

I might as well stop selling, because she isn't buying it. She knows me too well.

I'll never be a pub guy.

"From where *I'm* sitting, Mr. Day," she counters ominously, "you've only got two choices."

Shit, where the hell are they? Brendan's text this morning swore they'd be five minutes behind us, but Austen and I have been sitting here talking for over an hour with no sign of either of them. And they're not easy guys to miss.

The longer we wait, the guiltier I feel about Austen. She and I have known each other for a year now. We met at Indulgence, the popular multi-level spa and salon where I work as a massage therapist. She rents space in my section, offering facials and beauty regime counseling, as well as her own line of skincare products.

We've gotten to know each other between clients, and I genuinely like everything about her.

Which might explain why I'm feeling like an ass right now.

After all, I'm the one that invited her here on the pretext of brainstorming some ideas for her upcoming product parties. The truth is, this whole thing is a setup.

God, I hate matchmaking. Even thinking the word makes my skin crawl. Why did I let Brendan talk me into it?

Brushing the salt off my hands, I lean back, pretending an ease I don't feel as I continue to bluff my ass off. "These are mixed nuts, Austen. There are four different varieties to choose from in this bowl alone. If we add that to the amount of men currently wandering around this bar, each carrying a pair while trying to get your undivided attention—"

"Oh, you've moved on from fidgety to funny now. That's okay. I'll wait." She folds her arms fold gracefully on the table and stares me down, ignoring the half a dozen guys I've seen circling our table like hungry hyenas.

I can't blame them. Austen is gorgeous, with flawless dark skin, eternally perfect hair and a smile that makes everyone feel seen and special. None of her current admirers would guess that the lovely entrepreneur who always dresses like she's on her way to a fashion shoot also happens to have the soul of an inventor, a keen sense of humor—

And the tenacity of a gritty, B-movie vice cop when she thinks someone isn't being straight with her.

Damn, I'm so busted.

I sigh. "Okay, I'll bite—what two choices?"

"Confession or painful torture." Austen narrows her eyes suspiciously. "There's something going on with you, Miller Day. Confess."

In lieu of confession, I'd much rather be at home eating the empanadas currently going to waste in my fridge. Or maybe watching DIY channels on YouTube as I map out my scheduled house project for the weekend.

Look out, Property Brothers—I'm comin' for you with my mad home improvement skillz.

That's about as wild as my Friday nights usually get.

"Nothing's ever going on with me. Isn't that what they say on the Mean Girl side of the salon?"

The stylists at Indulgence aren't afraid to vocalize their disappointment when it comes to my lack of lifestyle. I don't dress to impress, I don't go clubbing, and I never have noisy, emotional breakups with hot boyfriends named Javier.

Miller Day, ladies and gentlemen—ruining gay stereotypes for catty women everywhere.

But I can't help who I am. I like to be comfortable, I'd rather eat nails than go to a gay club, and the only guy I've dated in the last year was a mildly attractive middle-school teacher named Robbie. Regrettable Robbie, who showed me once and for all why I was better off working on my house than ever dating again.

"Forget those idiots and focus, Miller. Your mind is wandering and I'm about to solve a mystery here."

I swallow my smile, take a drink of my water and nod obediently. "I'm all ears, Sherlock."

"I just texted my sister while you were over there gathering wool, and she confirmed that there is neither a surprise party nor a family gathering happening here in my honor." She points to my glass of sparkling water. "You rarely go out and when you do, you never drink, so bringing me to a bar—this bar in particular—instead of a diner or a donut shop to discuss taking my parties to the next level is highly suspect."

"Why this bar in particular?" I was just following

Brendan's orders.

And now I'm craving a donut.

"Are you serious?" From her expression I've said something so incredibly wrong it might start the apocalypse a week early. "Finn's pub. *Finn's.* As in Chief Finn, my brother's husband? As in Seamus Finn, the owner of this establishment and the guy who made my other brother, Thoreau, a partner in his micro brewing business? As in—"

"The man who married your big sister, Bronte?" I ask, feeling the need to smack my forehead on the table for not catching on sooner. "The one who owns that new boxing club you thought I should check out?"

Austen raises her hand as if asking for the check. "And he's finally awake."

Why didn't I put that together?

You've had other things on your mind.

I shake my head. "It didn't even occur to me. Everything is named Finn in this town. They can't all be related."

I could be wrong about that.

"You're wrong about that. And you *not* knowing makes the situation even more peculiar. I talk about them all the time, Miller. Some of them make the news on a regular basis, but even if they didn't, you work in the most popular spa in the city. My in-laws have been, hands down, the juiciest topic of conversation there for a while now."

I shrug helplessly. "You know I avoid gossip and current events whenever possible. If I didn't before, Fred's summer protest schedule was enough to depress me and put me off the news forever."

Using my teenage neighbor's civic responsibility as an excuse for not paying attention is low, even for me, but it makes Austen smile. "Well, I for one am glad that little rebel moved across the street from you. I like her, and you needed more adventure in your life. And friends. Not that I'm judging."

"I think I've hit my limit tonight," I say sincerely. "Any more adventure and I could have my first nervous breakdown. I'd rather skip it and hold out for that midlife crisis. I hear those are more fun."

"Which leads us to my final piece of evidence." Her expression is now the definition of smug. "You *are* nervous. Fidgety. You've been looking over your shoulder every five minutes since we got here, and I don't think it's because you have a thing for those dart-throwing firemen. The only conclusion a sane person could reach is that someone else is joining us, and you're feeling guilty about it. This feels like a setup. Blink twice if I'm right."

I blink.

Did I mention I knew this was a bad idea from the beginning? Just want to emphasize that for the record.

If you're wondering why I'm so anti-matchmaking, ask the two women who live next door to me. I've been the elderly couple's pet project since I moved in, but once they found some online blog about a gay man trying to get over his relationship dry spell, they got it into their heads that things were bad out there in dating land, and they had to take matters into their own hands when it came to finding my perfect match. Now, no matter how politely I try to dissuade them, they refuse to give up on their goal.

Those women are tenacious.

Believe me, I get it. People worry about my not having any fun. Or sex. Or a social life of any kind that could eventually lead to fun and sex. But even if I were interested, which I'm not, it's not like I have that many opportunities to do something about it.

The problem is that all of my coworkers, ninety-nine percent of my clientele and most of my friends are women. Oh, and I was raised by a single mom in an organic, testosterone-free environment.

Mom made sure I participated in most of the required rites of male passage—football tryouts, beer pong and peeing my name in the snow spring immediately to mind—but she and I both knew that if it weren't for the Internet, I'd never have learned about the gay birds and bees.

Seriously, she sent me a link when I was thirteen so she could be supportive but we wouldn't have to talk about it out loud.

Welcome to puberty! Think you're gay? Click here to learn more.

The one thing I couldn't learn from the privacy of my personal laptop was how to interact with men who wanted more than a professional backrub or my how-to on crown molding. Which is why, when the occasional delivery guy or some be-flannelled rando at the hardware store asks me out, I always manage to screw things up just enough to send them racing in the other direction.

Maybe my standards are too high. Maybe there are no good men left in this city.

Or maybe the only one I want is someone I can't

have, and I'm willing to do weird shit for him that makes me uncomfortable, even though he acted like a jackass the last time we saw each other.

No. That can't be it.

I run a hand through my shaggy mane and blow out a frustrated breath, upset with the entire situation. Brendan called and I caved, seeing an olive branch after months of silence instead of thinking it through. Now he's so late I'm starting to think he won't show at all. It wouldn't be the first time he's stood me up because something better came along. But I thought this time…

Damn you, Brendan.

Austen's touch gives me a jolt, and she squeezes my hand compassionately. "Who is he? The guy you're obsessing over."

I eye her warily. "Does your family descend from a coven of mind-reading witches or something?" At her glare, I raise my hands in surrender. "Just checking, Sherlock."

"Honey, you're easier to read than you know. You've been distracted for weeks now. Even a little sad, when you thought no one was paying attention. Then a few days ago things changed. You got all antsy and talkative, right around the time you invited me out. You even promised to go out to a place of *my* choosing next if I agreed. That should have been my first clue—you, voluntarily going out twice in the same month."

"I'll grovel if you need me to."

She squeezes my hand again. "Not necessary, as long as you promise you're not trying to hook me up with a guy you have the hots for. Friends come first, and I would never be okay with that kind of drama."

"No, it's not him." I shake my head in swift denial. "It's a mutual friend who wanted our help to meet you."

And now I've just admitted to setting her up *and* having the hots for Brendan. At least a life of crime was never on my bucket list.

Austen scoffs. "A man worth my time wouldn't use his friends as a shield or play high school games to get me. He'd come right up and introduce himself."

"Hey there, beautiful." The nearest bachelor hyena has decided to make his move after eavesdropping on our conversation.

Am I wearing a sign that says "Just a friend, mostly harmless and totally gay"?

It's hard not to take that personally, even if it is true. It's also true that I'm in better shape than he is and could probably dropkick him out the door if Austen asked me to. Still, it rankles.

Someone once told me I give off a harmless vibe, whatever that means.

That vibe might disappear if you wore something besides sweatpants and brushed your hair once in a while, Millie. Just saying.

The voice in my head occasionally channels my mother. It's awkward.

Before I can say a word, however, Austen responds to hyena number one without even looking in his direction. "No, thank you. Run along now, the adults are talking."

I'm not sure whether to feel sorry for the guy beating a fast retreat or applaud. I'm friends with a witch.

Since she sees right through me anyway, coming clean may be my only option.

"We had a falling-out a little while ago and took a step back." A Grand-Canyon-sized step that felt insurmountable at the time. "He reached out recently, asking me to help our friend get to know you without coming off like a player."

Austen frowns at that. "*Is* he a player?"

A few weeks ago, my answer would have been different. But now? "I wouldn't have agreed to it unless he'd personally convinced me that he was seriously interested. I'd never put you through this for any other reason."

At least that isn't a lie.

She nods thoughtfully. "So the one who reached out after stepping back—he's important to you?"

"Brendan?" For some reason the question surprises me.

Is Brendan Kinkaid important to me?

You could say that.

"We met when Mom was at the hospital for some tests about six years ago," I tell her, skimming over the details. "The two of them—mom and Brendan—just clicked. In one afternoon, he basically charmed her into unofficially adopting him. After that, whenever he was in town we were inseparable. Family dinners, weekly phone calls…he even sent flowers on Mother's Day. When she died a few years later, he was the one who helped get me through it."

He did a lot more than *help*. Anyone who's known me for more than three years knows how profoundly my mother's death affected me back then. She's the reason I decided to do what I do for a living—she'd always loved massages and I wanted to learn how to ease at least some of her pain. She's also the reason I saved up to buy the house. But complications from lupus got the best of her within days of my signing the closing paperwork. After that, everything I'd done or was planning to do felt pointless.

I shut down.

It was Brendan who moved me in when all I wanted was to curl into a ball and grieve. He invited the neighbors over to meet me. He's also the one who got me started on my never-ending home projects, giving me something to do so I wouldn't lose my mind.

In a very real way, Brendan saved me.

"He sounds like a good guy."

"He can be."

He's also the antithesis of me in every way. A straight, charismatic and overconfident daredevil who's spent more time in the air then on the ground, in a very literal sense. When he isn't flying a plane full of people across the country or over an ocean, he's finding new and improved ways to get himself in trouble. Women are always involved.

My mother called him precocious.

The last time *I* saw him I called him an asshole and kicked him out of my house along with Regrettable

Robbie (which was actually the night he earned that nickname).

For weeks afterward, I told myself I was right and it was time. Brendan and I were too different. We'd both cared for my mom, but I didn't approve of his irresponsible lifestyle and he thought I was wound too tight to have a successful relationship, sexual or otherwise.

Did you hate him for being right?

I push the question aside and focus on apologizing to Austen. "I should have known better, but by the time I got off the phone with Royal, *I* was nearly convinced he was perfect for you, and I disagree with matchmaking on a cellular level."

Royal had been persuasive and sincere. And he knew enough about her and what they had in common to surprise me. Both his and Austen's fathers are professors and bibliophiles. Both are from insanely large families—Royal is one of ten close-knit foster brothers and Austen has six siblings of her own, some of whom she sees on a daily basis. They're both confident, well-adjusted, funny and almost too attractive for their own good, inside and out.

Like I said, I was nearly convinced.

"But since they haven't bothered to show up," I continue with a scowl, "and no one's called to let me know what the hell is going on, none of those reasons matter anymore. So I'm taking the hint and retiring from the Cupid business, effective immediately. This was it. My first and last matchmaking assignment."

Austen sits up straighter, eyes wide with surprise. "The guy's name is Royal? You're sure? He wouldn't happen to be a pilot, would he? A big, muscular airline pilot with a loud laugh and a brother who married a guy he met in this very pub? *That's* who wanted to meet me?"

I send her a sheepish grin. "Small world, right? That's why we're here, for the record. He said it had to be here, since this is where he saw you for the first time."

Which, for Royal, sounded pretty damned romantic to me.

"Wow." She exhaled slowly, expression vaguely stunned. "Small world is right. Exactly how is the Rock-lookalike your friend? How did you meet him? He lives in New York, doesn't he?"

Wait, how does she know that? "He does, but he and Brendan work for the same airline. They've been buddies for years." I'm distracted by the strange look on her face. "Austen, are you *blushing*?"

"I never blush."

Until now, apparently.

Holy shit.

"Do you actually like Royal? Before you answer, remember that saying yes would really make me feel better about myself after dragging you out tonight under false pretenses."

She presses the back of her hand to her cheek. "I saw him at one engagement party, so I don't know him well enough to like him. To make you feel better, I'll admit I find him moderately attractive. And they weren't false pretenses. You've agreed to another friend date, and offered free massages at my first public meet up of the GPP next week. With your magic hands, I'll be in high demand in no time."

I don't remember agreeing to *that*, but I haven't been paying attention and she's willing to forgive me, so I'll take her word for it. "Are you sure you don't want to change the name while you still have time? 'Guinea Pig Party' was funny when it was just your family, but for the public it might be too…experimental. You're products are some of the best around, but most people aren't willing to volunteer their face to science."

"Fine." She rolls her eyes, which tells me I'm not the first person to point that out. "I'll think about it. So now that we've settled our business and we both know why we're really here, why don't you call your Brendan and see what's taking them so long?"

My Brendan.

I drop my gaze to the table to hide my reaction. "I'm not sure I want to know."

"You think they ditched us, don't you?" She sounds affronted, though I'm not sure if it's on my behalf or hers. I don't imagine anyone has ever ditched Austen Wayne before. "I thought these guys were your friends."

"They are." Note, I never said they're reliable. Or that they're not easily distracted by shiny objects, like flight attendants. I pull out my phone and scroll through my contacts. "Maybe there was a layover some—"

"Miller?" she interrupts me in a bemused tone that has me looking up again.

"What's wrong?"

"I think I have an idea about why they're late."

I almost smile. "Doing that witchy Sherlock thing again?"

"No," she shakes her head slowly, her attention glued

to the space over my shoulder. "Just using my eyes."

I turn in my chair and my jaw comes unhinged. Royal is trying to herd Brendan through the crowd toward our table, but he's not having much luck because Brendan is clearly hammered and stopping to drape himself over every warm body along the way.

What. The. Fuck.

Chapter Two

Go Home, Dick. You're Drunk

"Does he normally act like that?"

"Never." I slowly shove my phone back into my pocket, thinking this is what shock must feel like.

Royal gets to the table first and sends a look of genuine regret Austen's way. "Sorry, Miller. I tried to get him to stay in the car, but he's slippery." He leans closer, urgency in his usually jovial tone. "He was suspended. Grounded for two weeks over an incident he doesn't want to talk about."

I can't imagine anything Brendan would hate more than being grounded. "So you took him for a drink or ten without calling me? We've been waiting for over an hour."

"He was like this when I picked him up from the airport."

"He wasn't flying the plane, right?" Austen sounds about as horrified as I feel. "Tell me I'm right, even if you're lying, or I'll never make it to Paris."

"No." Royal's gaze locks on hers. "This time he was just a pain-in-the-ass passenger. And if you want to go to Paris, all you have to do is say the word. It's good to see you again, Austen."

She blushes. *Again.* "Back at you, Mr. Hale."

Despite my fascination, I miss the rest of their greeting because I'm already on my feet, hands flexing as Brendan weaves his way toward me.

My beautiful mess.

And he *is* a mess. His black hair is sticking out in some places and flattened in others, his brown eyes are bloodshot, and the strong line of his jaw is peppered with dark stubble. Stained and wrinkled as it is, he's still in his pilot's uniform and I know, if he were sober, he wouldn't go out like this in public.

While Brendan isn't serious about much, the man loves his uniform.

But even sloppy drunk, he's still every filthy dream

I've ever had come to life.

Months of separation might have made things worse instead of better, because just seeing him is making me ache. Actually ache, like parts of me are coming awake for the first time since he left and it hurts to feel them tingling and prickling with life again.

Now you know the real reason I don't date that much—I met the man who does it for me years ago, in a sad, sadistic place called the friend zone, and he's a hard damn act to follow.

"Miller Time!" Brendan shouts when he sees me. He throws his arms open wide, whacking a guy at the table closest to us.

"Hey," the man grumbles, rubbing the back of his head.

"Sorry, man," I apologize automatically, reaching for Brendan before he can cause any more damage. "I've got you, B."

Brendan's strong arms wrap around me and I'm instantly surrounded by the familiar scent of him. Well, his scent if he'd taken a bath in moonshine.

"You've got me." His face burrows into my neck, and it takes every bit of willpower to keep my erection in check.

Brendan is an affectionate friend—all manly hugging and ass slapping—and I do my best to ignore my reaction to his touch, because I've known for six years he's off limits. He's not into guys, and even if he swung that way, he's still the closest thing I have to family.

"I've missed you," he murmurs into my throat, his body leaning so heavily on mine I'm forced to bend my knees and brace.

"Why didn't you call me?" I ask, hoping he can't hear the vulnerability I'm feeling. "I was worried."

"I know. Fuck, I know I'm late. There was a dog. And this naked travel agent in my bed. I didn't know she was crazy when I gave her the key. And she was. She was *crazy,* Millie. You don't want to know."

No. I definitely don't want to know.

But at least I can always count on Brendan's mouth to remind my dick why it needs to stand down.

I really shouldn't think of his mouth and my dick in the same sentence.

Fortunately, I'm only sporting a semi since he mentioned the woman in his bed. The woman who had something he never once offered to me—a key to his condo.

How did he manage to find time for a drunken

quickie at his place before coming to the bar?

"I thought Royal picked you up at the airport."

"I did." The large and unfairly attractive Samoan who'd been talking quietly to Austen turns toward me when I mention his name. "We had to stop at his place first. In the category of perfect timing, we showed up at exactly the right moment for him to get evicted."

"What?" My head might start spinning soon. "He was suspended *and* evicted? Today?"

"Right?" Brendan says indignantly, reaching up to tug on my hair playfully. "The evil condo landlord says I can't have wild orgies on the premises. Even when I'm not there to enjoy them. Says he already gave me a warning about it last week, but I didn't get that either. I was away in London."

Austen's chuckle sounds uncomfortable. "Is this conversation supposed to be making sense?"

"Only if you speak drunken jet lag." I tighten my hold on Brendan, trying to evade his roving hands. "Come on, B. I think we all need some fresh air."

Brendan shakes his head aggressively, almost dislodging himself from my grip. "We just got here. Royal is in love and we're his wingmen, remember? We have to get these two crazy kids together so he'll stop talking to me about his *feelings*. It's a mission of mercy."

My face flames in sympathetic embarrassment as I look over at Austen and Royal. "I think he thought he was whispering."

"Don't worry about it, big guy." Austen looks up at an embarrassed Royal and gives him a wink. "I think it's kind of cute, you calling in reinforcements."

A few minutes ago she thought it was a high-school move, but I'll die before I remind her. "A little help here?"

Royal takes over for me, holding Brendan upright with one arm the size of a tree trunk so Austen can gather her things before we head out to the parking lot.

"I'm assuming you won't need a ride home," she says as we follow the two men to a rented Range Rover and watch Royal lift Brendan into the backseat as if he were a child.

"No. I really am sorry about this, Austen. He isn't usually like this."

"Everybody has a rough day now and then." She slips her arm around my waist and squeezes. "Stop apologizing. I actually had fun. And I'm not judging anyone. I think you're pretty wonderful, so I don't imagine you would care about him as much as you do if he wasn't a good man."

I squeeze back gratefully and then notice Royal sending me a look that tells me to get my "wonderful" self lost so he can make his move.

Speaking of high school.

"I'll call you tomorrow," I promise, reaching for the front passenger door.

Royal blocks me with one massive hand. "That seat is occupied. Anyway, I need you on babysitting duty. On the way here, your friend tried to hug me from the back seat and nearly ran us off the road."

My friend? But I nod and head to the back, climbing in beside my now-scowling charge. "What's *that* look for?"

"I don't need a damn babysitter," he mutters petulantly.

"That's a relief. I retired from that career over twelve years ago—the pocket change isn't worth the pain and suffering." I gird my loins and reach across his lap for the seatbelt. "Now let's get you buckled in."

His big hand cups the back of my head, holding me in place while he plays with my hair.

I clench my teeth to fight back a moan. He has to

know what he's doing, right? Has to know how I'm positioned? What this would look like to anyone watching?

He's affectionate, remember? Even when he's sober. It doesn't mean anything.

I can't resist looking down at the lap I'm hovering over, but what I see is just as confusing as it is arousing. Brendan's dick is hard, long and perfectly outlined against the dark fabric of his dress pants. I mean, I knew he was built—six years is a long time to resist checking out your sexy friend's junk, and I'm not vying for sainthood—but I've never had the opportunity to study it up close and in person before.

My ass clenches instinctively as I imagine what he would feel like inside me. I've bought a few dildos over the years for those times when my hand wasn't getting the job done. And yes, most of them were used while thinking of him, and one might even be named Brendan Two. But the original is definitely thicker.

Did I mention he was hard?

Why is *that* happening? I could have sworn I'd heard drinking made it difficult to get it up.

It's not about you. It can't be. Seatbelt, asshole. Remember who he is.

Family. Friend. Heterosexual.

Off limits.

"I was looking forward to tonight," Brendan says, completely oblivious to my silent perusal. "You and I haven't been out in years."

I was too. But there's no way we can have a coherent conversation about anything right now, so I just buckle him up and put some much-needed distance between us instead.

"I remember the last time I took you out drinking," he muses, eyes narrowed as if trying to focus on me. "You weren't one full glass in before you started singing at the top of your lungs. I wish I'd recorded it. You know you made a few of the girls at that bachelorette party cry?"

Of course he didn't record it. He was too busy consoling the maid of honor in a bathroom stall while I embarrassed myself in public.

It's one of the reasons I don't drink. Sad cabaret singer is *not* a good look for me.

"They weren't crying because of my voice," I'm compelled to remind him. "It was my song list."

Never sing old Roberta Flack classics to a bunch of women with romance on their minds and five empty margarita pitchers on their table.

What? I know old songs. And my mom loved Roberta.

Brendan is still staring at me. I've never seen him give me that particular look before and it's freaking me out.

He looks like he wants to kiss you.

Lies.

"Exactly how many of those tiny bottles of airline hooch did you knock back to get this wasted?" I ask.

He laughs softly, reaching into his pocket and pulling out a small sealed bottle. "You want my last one? I'll give it to you if you sing for me again."

I frown and snatch it out of his hand before he can toss it back. "My singing days are over. And any more of that and we'll have to spend the night in an emergency room instead of home in bed."

Brendan licks his lips and smiles wickedly. "Trying to get me into bed already, huh?"

Is it hot in here?

In an act of divine dispensation, Royal opens the driver's side door and climbs in, distracting Brendan before I can think of a response that doesn't start with *Yes, please.*

"Did you kiss her?" Brendan asks curiously. "You were gone long enough to read her that book of sonnets I saw in your carryon."

"I don't know what you're talking about." Royal shakes his head as he pulls out of the parking lot. "I walked her to her car because I'm a gentleman."

"Hah." Brendan laughed. "Tell that to Italy. Oh wait, you can't go back to Italy for at least a year."

"I'm going to let that pass, because despite your making me late and causing a scene, she still gave me her number."

Austen, you minx.

I have to admit, I really like Royal. Since his brother got married, he's been stopping by to visit on a regular basis so I've gotten to know him a little better. And now that I've seen them side by side, imagining a Royal and Austen love match is not that much of a stretch.

Am I the first successful gay virgin Cupid? Does Guinness keep records of that kind of thing?

"He's still mad at me," Brendan whisper-shouts. "Because I cockblocked him in Dallas. Even if he did get her number."

I pat him on the knee. "Not *in Dallas*. *With Austen*. And I'm sure he'll forgive you eventually."

Royal snorts from the front seat.

"Do *you* forgive me?" Brendan clumsily unlatches his seatbelt and turns his body toward mine, leaning his head on my shoulder. "I cockblocked you too, didn't I? Fuck, I'm a fucking cockblocker. I *hate* cockblockers."

Please, Lord. Make him stop saying cockblocker.

"It's all good, okay? We're fine. Bros before…whatever. We're good."

His fingers tug at the fabric covering my thigh. "Are you still seeing him?"

The last thing I want to talk about is Robbie. "Not since that night, no."

He snuggles closer, his lips pressed against my neck again. "You smell good, Millie. You always smell so good."

"It's the massage oil," I say uncomfortably. I don't wear cologne or body spray and I stick with unscented soap because I'm in a small, confined space with clients all day long. But the oil I use gives off a pleasant, relaxing aroma that lingers.

"No, it's you. You smell like fresh air and sunshine, Day." His hand moves higher on my thigh and I grip it in mine to stop him from discovering my reaction to his cuddling. He sniffs again. "And wood. You smell like wood. Working on another project for the house?"

"Always," I say through gritted teeth. "Cedar deck."

"Good choice. I've always wanted one of those."

This is torture. I need to phone a friend.

"How long are you in town, Royal?" I ask a little too loudly.

He looks in the rearview mirror, laughter in his eyes as he takes in Brendan clinging to me like I'm his damn security blanket.

"In an interesting plot twist, I've decided to use some of my vacation days to torture my brother and check out a few real estate possibilities. Based on tonight's events, about two weeks, I'd say."

"Two weeks," Brendan grumbles against my shoulder.

But Royal's words have grabbed my interest. "Are you getting a place in town?"

His boulder-sized shoulders shrug. "My parents and a few of my brothers are still in Washington, but I realized recently that I have more friends here than I do back home, or in New York after years of living there. Brendan, JD, Carter. You. And those Finns are entertaining as hell. I was thinking it's time I slowed things down. Stopped traveling the world so much and did a little nesting."

Nesting? Royal Hale? The only man Brendan has ever claimed is more of a ladies' man than he is?

It dawns on me that Royal didn't mention Austen. Her absence on the list is *so* transparent and suspicious, I bet her witchy Sherlock senses are tingling way over on the other side of town.

Is he really that interested? Nesting level interested?

"That's great," I say sincerely as Brendan nuzzles behind my ear and hums against my pulse. "If you need any help with that, let me know. I could use another guy in the neighborhood."

Brendan shouldn't be the only man I hang out with. That's weird, right? And I miss him too much when he's gone.

"I'll introduce you to my brother and his husband. They've finally decided to make those Dry Spell Diaries of his into a book, so he's a little hard to live with these days, but he's always a riot. You'll like JD."

"Dry Spell?" My grip on Brendan's hand tightens until he makes a sound of vague, drunken protest. "Your brother is the advice columnist? I thought his name was Green."

"It is. We all have the last names we came to Rick

and Matilda with. It was confusing for the postal service and family stationary was out, but it worked for us." Royal's eyes narrow on me in the mirror. "Why do you look so shocked? Did you two date? You should tell me now, because Carter can be a little possessive of my brother."

"No," Brendan growls, trying to tug me closer.

What the hell?

"My neighbors are fans, that's all," I say weakly. "Big fans. I've never met JD."

I've never met him or dated him, but Royal's brother is the reason my neighbors keep trying to fix me up. The reason I hate matchmaking so much I almost didn't agree to come out tonight.

Small world.

We finally pull up to my two-story house and I instantly set to work disentangling our limbs so I can get Brendan inside where he can sleep it off.

He doesn't want to let go.

"I'll get his luggage," Royal calls when I've finally got him on his feet and walking toward the front door. I nod, pulling the key chain out of my pocket one-handed.

Once inside, I flip on the lights and a part of me automatically relaxes, tension I wasn't even aware of disappearing in an instant.

Home.

Away from the noise and crowds, this place is clean and peaceful and exactly what I need. Every brick and square of travertine tile has been repaired or installed by yours truly. Every picture on the wall, including a few my mother painted before she died, is framed and hung with care.

After a lifetime of one-bedroom apartments with leaky faucets and warped linoleum, this might as well be a mansion.

It's too big for one person.

Brendan picks that moment to stop clinging and strides into my living room, dropping on my couch with a thump.

Déjà vu.

Royal curses in the foyer, and when I turn to help him with his load, I get another surprise.

The luggage is alive.

That must be what was in the front seat.

"Um, Royal? Is that an actual dog?"

"In theory." He sets the crate down and chuckles. "It looks more like a baby Ewok to me, but what do I know? I don't even have real plants at my apartment."

It's a Yorkshire terrier. Bigger than a teacup, but not by much. "How—"

"Beats me. Unless he swiped it from some Paris Hilton type or it's the heir to a canine fortune, we shouldn't do jail time for keeping him for the night. He even came with his own pads to pee on."

"Pads?"

Royal chuckled. "You see the size of that thing? A hawk could carry him away for supper if you let him roam the backyard unattended."

Good point.

"If you invite me back for breakfast, we can ask Kinkaid about it in the morning. I'd love to get a front row seat to the hangover he's in for."

I bet he would. "Sounds like a party," I say automatically. "You're invited."

What am I going to do with a dog for the night? Will he eat my shoes? Furniture cushions? Empanadas? It's not like I can kick him out, though—he's too ridiculously cute and the way he's snoring is so loud for such a little thing it makes me smile. "I'll take care of them." The man *and* his Ewok.

Royal hesitates. "You okay with Brendan staying with you for a few days? At least until he sorts out his condo situation or gets another place? If not, JD and Carter have the room—"

"I have room too," I say gruffly. "It's not like he hasn't crashed here before."

"He'll definitely be more comfortable here," Royal agrees easily. "TMI, but my brother and his husband can be a little loud."

I glance up at him and bite my lip. "So was it really an orgy? At the condo?"

Royal's eyes widen dramatically as he nods. "I've seen some shit tonight. I might be emotionally scarred."

"I doubt that. What I don't get is why the landlord kicked him out when it was obvious he'd just got back in town."

Royal smirks. "That was personal. I hear he got turned away from the party twice. That's enough to make any man vindictive. I suppose Brendan could fight it if he wanted to, but he didn't seem all that interested when we left."

"Twice?"

"Kimmy—that's the travel agent—asked for a place to crash and ended up having multiple parties of the extremely loud and incredibly naked variety, which is probably why she didn't want to stay in a hotel. She thought he was a pervert."

When we laugh, Brendan shouts from the living room, "Stop mocking my pain."

Royal shakes his head and lays a monster paw on my shoulder. "Thanks for bringing Austen tonight. It might not have gone as planned, but you really came through. I owe you one."

I smile, because he really does. "You can help with the deck tomorrow. And when you get your new place, we'll go plant shopping. Maybe we can bring her along."

His expression brightens and then he waves, heading back out into the night.

After I lock the door, I walk back to the living room to see Brendan's six-foot frame sprawled across my couch. He's kicked off his shoes and is in the process of unbuttoning his shirt. "I've never been so ready for a day to be over."

Give me strength.

Without a word, I fast-walk my way to the kitchen to grab a large glass of water and some aspirin, then let the dog out of his crate and lay one of the blue pads down in case he needs to relieve himself. The little dude wakes up immediately and does his business without a peep before returning to the crate and curling up on his pale pink pillow.

"Ridiculous," I whisper, shaking my head. "That should be your name."

In the living room, I hand Brendan the water and aspirin. Then I pick up his shoes, placing them side by side at the end of the couch, and fold his dirty shirt to keep my hands busy while he guzzles down the water like he's been in the desert for a year.

"Do you like your present?" he finally asks.

Present?

He sets the glass on my coffee table and, before I can put down a coaster or ask him what he's talking about, he wraps his fingers around my wrist and tugs.

I tumble on top of him. "Brendan what the—"

His kiss cuts off my shout of surprise.

I'd like to say its shock that keeps me from immediately rejecting the press of his lips, but when mine part for his stroking tongue on a whimper, I know it's a lie. I don't want to reject it. Right or wrong, I can't deny myself the pleasure of knowing what it's like to kiss this man I've wanted for so long.

Brendan's hungry moans and the deep, demanding thrust of his tongue set me on fire. His stubble scrapes against my skin as he tilts his head and I shudder against him, so aroused I can hardly breathe.

Air is overrated. Don't stop.

"Millie…" His hands burrow beneath my sweatpants and boxer briefs, gripping the cheeks of my ass and rocking me against him. "Missed you."

Millie.

The old nickname sends a jolt through my body, and so does the hard, heavy feel of his cock rocking against mine. He wants this? Me?

Think, Miller. That doesn't make sense.

I push away from him and try to climb off the couch. "You're drunk, Brendan. Really fucking drunk and you don't know what you're doing. Let me go."

He holds on tighter, one hand at the back of my neck and the other slipping between us to wrap around my thickening erection. "Please. It's okay. I know. I know and I need you…"

I need you.

He lifts his head off the couch to kiss me again, and then starts to stroke my shaft. When his thumb slides over the head to gather the moisture already beading at the tip, I cry out in surprised pleasure. He bites my upper lip before sucking on my tongue and my entire body responds, hips thrusting greedily into his fist.

I don't do this. One or two men have gotten to this point in my lifetime. Tried to touch me like this. Usually my brain is too busy—

"Oh God," I moan, my eyes nearly rolling back as his grip tightens around me. "I'm close."

Close because it's Brendan's hand. His mouth on mine. I've always wanted it. I've been waiting for it.

He knows.

I break away from the kiss to look down, needing to see what he's doing that's turning my body inside out. My blood pounds in my ears as I watch myself fucking his strong, perfect fist. "Christ. What are we doing?"

"Just give it to me," he mutters, watching with me, eyes dark and unfocused. "I need to see it. Need to know what you look like when you come."

My spine arches in an unexpected wave of pleasure at his words. No session with my own hand has ever been this good. Nothing has ever been this good. I can't hold back.

Brendan.

The shout that escapes my throat is raw and ragged as jets of come land on his knuckles, his flat stomach and chest. I can't stop fucking his hand, desperate to hold onto this feeling, the friction causing sparks to shoot up my spine and out from my fingertips.

Can't stop. Don't ever stop.

He pulls me down on top of him and now I'm the one burying my face in his neck, unable to believe I'm not dreaming. I have to be dreaming, right? I would never make this kind of mistake in real life.

He would never want me in real life.

He still doesn't. He's so drunk he's barely coherent.

I stiffen and his arms tighten around me. "Wait a second. Don't freak out."

But I am.

"You're not gay," I whisper. "You don't want this."

I took advantage of the situation. I'm *that* guy.

"That's not true anymore," he says, his words slurring together now. "Don't send me away again, Millie. Please."

The plea makes my heart hurt. I know today must have destroyed him. Being suspended from the only thing he loves, and then kicked out of his place when he was down.

This is my friend and he's hurting.

This is your friend who sleeps with women when he isn't blind drunk and jerking you off.

I take a deep breath, fortifying myself and trying to

ignore the aftershocks of arousal pulsing through me as I raise my head to look him in the eye.

His are already closed, his features too slack and relaxed for him to be pulling my leg. His soft snores instantly sync with the sounds his ridiculous dog is making and I'm not sure whether to laugh or cry.

"Why am I not surprised?"

I whack him lightly on the chest, then reach up to give his jaw a shake. Nothing.

The bastard fell asleep on me. Well, under me. And if I want to get technical he didn't fall so much as crash. He's out cold.

I slide off him until I'm on my knees beside the couch with my sweats around my thighs and my heart trying to hammer its way out of my chest.

What did I just do?

"That's not true anymore."

And what the hell did *that* mean?

CHAPTER THREE

A Brunch of Regrets

Brendan

That moment, right before consciousness hits, when you realize you're going to regret waking up?

Shit, I think I'm there.

At least the conversation—the one I wouldn't be overhearing if I were in my own bed where I belong—is taking care of the monster hard-on I woke up with.

"Is it, you've got another *think* coming or another *thing* coming?"

"People usually say thing, but think is the original colloquialism."

"Fred, stop showing off. You know how much Diane

hates crosswords."

"I really do. And words like colloquialism. But I never welch on a bet."

"We know, sweet cheeks. Now let's all keep it down so we don't wake up Miller's sexy flyboy, hmm? They obviously had a busy night, if you know what I mean."

"Cut it out, Heather, or I'll eat that biscuit you've got your eye on. You all know Brendan is just a friend."

Just a friend.

It's that voice, deep and smooth and currently laced with barely concealed discomfort that fully drags me from oblivion.

Not that I haven't missed him like hell, but what's Miller doing here with the estrogen posse?

Use your head, flyboy. Do you know where you are right now? If you think Miller would be cooking for his neighbors at the condo he calls Casa de Horndog, you've got another think *coming.*

I wish permanent memory loss came with this whopper of a migraine I drank myself into. Unfortunately, things are already starting to come back to me.

Fuck my life.

Too late. Looks like I already took care of that

myself.

After a few forceful blinks to unglue my eyelids and face the music, I'm confronted by a pair of cartoonishly large brown eyes. "Huh. That's new."

There's a small, furry growth on my chest that wasn't there yesterday. And it's staring at me with an expression that strongly resembles disappointment.

What the hell, dog? I don't even know you.

I swear silently, managing to get myself into an upright position while carefully settling the judgmental ankle biter down on the cushion beside me. He's solid in my grip so it's safe to assume he's not a hallucination. "I'll get to you later."

He wags his stub of a tail agreeably.

I need a minute to take stock of my situation, because so far it's not looking so good. Embarrassment aside, my stomach is roiling, my eyeballs are hot and dry, and my aching neck and knees are telling me that blacking out on a couch is a younger man's game.

Public Service Announcement: At thirty-five, hangovers come with a crick in the neck, a sour stomach and a bonus shot of self-recrimination. The more you fucking know.

"You can all relax now. It lives," Miller says wryly

from the kitchen, his words echoing through the throbbing canyon of suck where my head used to be.

"Royal. He drove us back here, right?"

He'll be pissed at me, I'm sure. I'm surprised I didn't wake up with a dick drawn on my face again. I scrub my jaw self-consciously, hoping he couldn't get his hands on a permanent marker.

I hear a woman scoff from the kitchen and look over to see the familiar faces of Miller's next-door neighbors. Other than their personalities, it's hard to tell the two apart. Both women have short, blonde hair and a penchant for tie-dye, and rarely do you see one without the other.

When the sixty-something couple basically adopted Miller as soon as he moved in, I was relieved. He'd just lost his mother and the way they fussed over him as we got him settled gave me hope that he'd be okay when I wasn't around.

Then about a year ago they started nagging him to date, determined to find him his perfect partner. Okay, Diane wanted perfect—Heather just wanted Miller to get laid.

I like Heather.

"Memory loss. How convenient."

Diane, I tolerate.

"Not really," I say, as if she's talking to me instead of about me. "Just getting my bearings."

I stand up and stretch, recalling more of the worst day of my life. Flying home with my tail between my legs and two weeks suspension to suffer through while the airline *reviews the incident.*

I definitely remember the incident.

I also have a vague recollection of walking through the door of my condo and finding my old pal Kimmy throwing the kind of party you'd only see in a private dungeon, complete with an actual cage where my coffee table used to be.

I can't begin to fathom how they got that thing up the elevator.

The details are a little fuzzy after that. All I know was there was a lot of nudity, a lot of yelling from the little guy who held my lease, and before I knew it, I'd been evicted and told I would be notified when I could pick up my things.

No spare key goes unpunished.

Thanks, Kimmy.

At any other time in my life I might have cajoled the landlord into giving me a warning by finding him a willing partner, and then joined the party myself. I've never had a problem with a little healthy debauchery, and I've rarely taken the moral high ground in lieu of getting laid.

I used to joke that there wasn't much difference between a pilot's life and a pirate's—taming the wind, thriving on danger and traveling the world in search of adventure and booty. Emphasis on the booty, of course.

Blackbeard didn't have tempting flight attendants offering kinky refreshments to their captain on the red eye, but other than that, the resemblance is uncanny.

Flying pirate that I am, I'll let that tan line on the third finger of your left hand slide without judgment. Want to invite a few of your friends to my hotel room or join me in the plane's tiny bathroom for an official meeting of the mile-high club? I have no problem with that. The friendly skies have always been good to me, and I've done my best to reciprocate.

The problem with the pirate comparison is that there aren't that many who are famous for retiring with their treasured booty intact. And unless it's a fairy tale, none of them fall in love and settle down. You're a pirate until you die—from a flesh would or syphilis—or until the crew mutinies. The end.

Royal and I both came to the same realization at about the same time when we met up in London on a layover. Pilots? Always. But we no longer want to be pirates. We want something more out of life. In Royal's case, he wants a woman who happens to work with my…with Miller.

I rub the knots in my neck, the discomfort almost a relief. I deserve to be in some pain. Not just because I embarrassed my friends and came on too strong with Miller, no doubt confusing the shit out of him. But also because yesterday I was attacked, suspended and evicted all in one day, and my reaction to all of it was mild irritation and relief.

Relief. How fucked up is that?

"Here." Miller was suddenly beside me, handing me a large glass of freshly squeezed orange juice and two Advil.

"Bless you, hangover angel."

"Shut it. I'm planning on giving you hell later for passing out in the middle of our discussion last night."

Discussion. Is that what he's calling it?

He leans closer and murmurs, "They showed up before I could cancel. It's Saturday."

"Right. I remember Saturday brunch," I sigh,

popping the pills into my mouth and swallowing them dry. "Ari made the best mimosas."

Aurelia Day, Miller's mom, started the tradition when he was a kid as a way to make sure her shy son socialized and had a supportive community around him. Miller's obviously keeping it going in her memory.

Though I wouldn't know, since I haven't made it to one in a while. My schedule isn't what anyone would call regular, and Miller hates being stood up.

"I didn't think you'd want one this morning."

"One? Oh, a mimosa." I grimace, taking the glass of juice gratefully. "You're right. This is exactly what I need. And I appreciate knowing you didn't invite the neighborhood over just to gawk at my pain."

"It's not your pain they're gawking at." Miller slings one of my old faded t-shirts over my shoulder. "You left this in the laundry room the last time you were here. It's clean."

I watch his gaze flick back to my bare chest and try not to smile. I don't think the lesbian couple is that interested in my charms, but I don't bother pointing out the obvious.

It's a good sign, I think as I slip the shirt over my head. At least I know we both still like what we see.

Miller was never that subtle about his attraction to me. I told myself it was just my ego that was flattered, explaining away all the times I made sure he got an eyeful.

But even when I was deluding myself, I was reciprocating. It's an impossible task, not noticing Miller Day. Everything about him draws the eye. Olive skin with a smattering of freckles, a full upper lip that gives him a permanent, almost feminine pout, and a messy fall of thick hair that's a natural mix of blond, brown and auburn. His eyes can't commit to a color either—sometimes they're hazel, and sometimes they glimmer like gold.

For some reason I've never been able to understand, he thinks his looks make him invisible or easy to dismiss, but he's anything but. All those features that shouldn't go together, added to his sculpted five-eleven frame, make him unique.

Unforgettable.

I've always had a thing for his hands too. Strong from spending his days massaging wealthy women into a state of gelatinous bliss, and calloused from all the work he's done on his house.

I've had dreams about those hands on me, complete

with happy endings and Miller's oiled up body rubbing against mine as we both took out our tension on each other.

Shut that train down, buddy.

I need to stop fantasizing and focus on getting him alone so I can do some damage control. Hopefully brunch is almost over.

I'm taking another sip of juice, my attention riveted to the dimple on his chin, when I hear a high-pitched bark. I forgot about him. "What's with the dog?"

Miller's changeable eyes widen in disbelief. "You don't remember your dog?"

What else don't you remember?

I know that's what he's thinking.

Instead of giving in to the temptation to recount every detail of our kiss, I glance over at the Yorkie, who's currently giving Miller a look of pure adoration and sneezing excitedly at being included in the conversation. I get a hazy image of a woman in leopard print handing me a carrier in exchange for a wad of cash.

Did I buy a damn dog last night? It doesn't sound like me. I lease a furnished condo on a monthly basis. I don't own a car. I've never bought a plant.

But I sort of remember purchasing a pampered pup in

an airport.

I was trying to find the right gift for Miller. Something that said "I'm sorry we fought, I'm a prick, it won't happen again" along with "I know I've been straight for years, but I think we should have sex and move in together." Something that was a promise as much as an apology.

And thanks to the woman ditching her rich boyfriend and running off to Rome with an underwear model, I got first dibs on a sentient hairball.

Airports have everything.

"I'm pretty sure he's *your* dog." I stop and laugh wryly. "Should have said it with a card, I guess. But at least I didn't steal him. I think I even have his pedigree papers in my suitcase."

The dog came with papers. I wish I could remember how much I paid.

Miller looks down at the dog and nibbles his lip. I know that nibble. He wants to be excited, but he's not sure if he should. "You got me a dog?"

"Best apology present ever," Heather laughs from her perch in the kitchen.

"I like flowers," Diane muttered, glaring down at her crossword.

I keep forgetting we have an audience.

Miller shifts awkwardly and takes a not-so-subtle step back, putting more space between us—which is the opposite of what I want.

"We can talk about this later," he says. "Go splash some water on your face while I make you a plate. Royal's on his way over and you'll handle him better after you eat something."

I follow him to the kitchen first to set my glass in the sink, glancing at Heather and Diane as I do it. "Sorry for interrupting, ladies."

"I can't imagine getting drunk enough to forget buying a dog. You're like a character from that Hangover movie," says a gangly teenager who's leaning on the island's butcher-block.

Doesn't Miller know anyone with a filter?

"I'm not that bad," I say, rubbing the back of my neck. "That dog is small, but I'd never forget a tiger."

Miller nudges me with his shoulder. "Say hello to my new neighbor, Fred."

Fred has a shaved head underneath a backwards baseball cap. A purple tank top with the words Resist across the chest, a utili-kilt and a pair of combat boots with pink laces finish off the ensemble. That look is definitely saying something, but I'm not in any shape to translate it. "Nice to meet you, Fred. I'm Brendan."

The teen smirks. "Oh, I know who you are. I've heard a lot about you since my sister and I moved in across the street. They didn't mention you were bangin'."

Heather frowns at Fred. "You heard me call him sexy, didn't you? Isn't that what banging means?"

Diane looks up from her paper and rolls her eyes. "Why would we mention it? He's not exactly our type."

You're not exactly mine either, Grouchy.

"Thank you, Fred," I say, my smile as charming as I can make it with the constant pounding in my skull. "I don't feel all that banging at the moment, but I appreciate the compliment."

"You're tall too." Fred abruptly crouches to shuffle through a giant bag covered in brightly colored pins. "I have a sign I bet would get more visibility if—"

"Fred," Miller says firmly. "The enthusiasm is commendable, but Brendan had a rough night and he's still recovering. You can't recruit him today."

"Fine," Fred grumbles, shrugging and reaching for another strip of bacon. "I'll do it tomorrow."

My stomach growls, and Miller grabs me by the

shoulders and turns me toward the downstairs bathroom. "Go on. After you eat you can decide whether you want to save the world or help me build my deck."

His touch disappears and I instantly regret the loss. "Off the top of my aching head, I'm going with deck."

There's no way I'm leaving Miller's side until we have that talk.

If it goes well, I'm not going anywhere for a while.

The laughter and teasing arguments follow me then fade as I round the corner. I rub my neck again. I'll need a hot shower soon to get rid of this knot. Maybe next time I'll get him a more comfortable couch instead of a dog.

Locking the bathroom door behind me, I take a deep breath and look in the mirror. "Nice."

Unless banging means I look like shit on toast, I'm thinking Fred needs to add a pair of colorful glasses to his outfit. *Her* outfit? Jesus, am I getting too old to tell?

I turn the cold tap and dunk as much of my head in the sink as I can, but the icy water does little to alleviate the need that started pumping through me as soon as Miller put his hands on me.

I'm still getting used to it. This desire I have to fuck my best friend blind.

And yes, I'm an idiot who fought it to the bitter end, but it's definitely here to stay.

I don't throw the word love around that much. My parents were in love, but it turned to hate fast enough and they started using me as a tool to hurt each other on a regular basis. That was my status quo for years, until my mother died. She loathed her husband so much that she drew her final breath, not holding the hand I was trying to offer in comfort, but cursing his name and giving me her stocks in his company for one last poke in the eye.

That's why I was in the hospital that day. She'd wanted me at her side when she passed. I sat there, struggling to feel more than obligation and pity, but that was all I had left for the woman who'd never once told me she loved me.

We weren't exactly a happy family.

But then something happened. I turned a corner in that sterile hallway and saw, through an open door, Aurelia and Miller Day arguing with a dismissive nurse. They were sitting close together on the hospital bed, hands tightly entwined as they asked how much longer they'd be waiting for the doctor to explain her test results.

The love between them was palpable. Recognizable, even to a sorry bastard like me. And in that moment, I knew I wanted to know them. Help if I could. Maybe it was only to shake off my guilt at feeling so little for the woman who'd given birth to me, but I walked in there like I owned the place, said a few choice words to the nurse that sent her running, and introduced myself.

I've never experienced anything like it before or since, and over the years the only way I could explain it to myself was that there are some people who are just supposed to be in your life. Through fate or coincidence, I found them, and I knew within minutes of meeting them that I didn't want to let them get away. Miller and his mother were my people.

I think I loved him right away. I didn't question it, didn't doubt it, but I never in a million years imagined it could change into something different. Something that wasn't as pure as what I felt in that hospital room.

On that day I knew that I was as straight as they come and Miller was going to be my family.

Looking back, I can see now that my feelings were already starting to change before his mother died. I just didn't realize what was happening until I stormed into Miller's living room to find him half-naked and making out with another man on the couch.

A brisk knock jolts me out of my stupor.

"Brendan? If you're hiding, they're gone now. And your food's getting cold."

As Miller's steps fade, I look at myself in the mirror again, pushing my wet hair off my face and reaching for one of the extra toothbrushes that Miller always has on hand in case of emergency.

We're finally alone. I better make this count.

I find a plate with sizzling bacon, hot biscuits and jam waiting for me on the counter and smile. No eggs. He always remembers. "Thanks."

He sets down a fresh glass of juice and studies me as I slide onto the now-empty stool. "How's your head doing?"

"Better." I take a bite of crisp bacon and close my eyes, savoring the taste. "This helps."

"Good."

He's silent while I eat, wiping down the counter a little too vigorously for me not to notice. I drop my last bite of bacon on the floor next to the waiting Yorkie and reach for a napkin to wipe the grease off my hands. "So who did the dynamic duo try to set you up with while I was sleeping?"

Miller pauses, his lips quirking. "Diane's dermatologist. She went in to check on a mole and he liked the picture of me she had on her phone."

Fucking Diane. "Interested?"

He shakes his head firmly and I relax.

"Too bad," I lie. "And this new neighbor? What's Fred short for?"

Fredrick? Winifred?

His eyes meet mine and the knowing laughter in them makes me grin. "Fred hasn't decided on gender yet, but we're allowed to use the pronoun *she* when referring to her, since we're too old to grasp the vernacular of her generation's sexuality."

I laugh and shake my head. "She said that? She's like twelve, isn't she?"

"Fifteen. A very mature and intelligent fifteen." Miller's smile dims. "She's been through a lot. Most of it on her own since her sister—who as far as we can tell is her only legal guardian—basically dropped her off at the rental house across the street, vanishing for long periods of time to hang out with her boyfriend. We hardly see that one. Heather and I take turns making sure Fred has groceries and money for clothes."

"Damn."

Of course Miller is looking out for her. His mother had a habit of collecting strays as well—I'm a prime example of that—and he's more like her than he knows.

"Oh, about your dog." Miller reaches for my plate but I lightly slap him away and get up to put it in the dishwasher.

"Your dog," I say firmly.

"I found his papers in your suitcase while I was putting your clothes away. Dresser in the second guest room, by the way. Did you know his name? Is that why you bought him?"

He unpacked my clothes while I was sleeping? That's the best news I've heard all morning.

He's assuming I'll stay. He wants me to stay. I'm almost thankful to kinky Kimmy for getting me evicted.

"Well?"

Right. The dog's name. "No idea what his name is. Snuggles? Lamby Pie?"

"Dix Balzack. The third."

The plate wobbles in my hand and Miller grabs it with practiced ease, sliding it into the dishwasher in a smooth move I'd applaud if I weren't in shock on the dog's behalf.

"Dicks Ballsack?"

"Balzack. The third."

"What kind of—the third? That means there are two other dogs out there with the same name?"

Miller meets my gaze and in seconds we're both leaning against the counter and laughing our asses off. The poor dog racing in a circle and yipping doesn't seem to care that we're laughing at his frank-and-beans moniker. Either he's got a good sense of humor, or he's hoping I'll drop more bacon.

"We'll keep Dix," he finally tells me. "I wanted to name him Ridiculous anyway, so I can work with it. But I'm taking him to the vet in a few hours and I'm not mentioning Balzack. We'll take that to our graves."

We.

My laughter fades, but I'm still smiling down at him. "Deal."

I think I stare long enough to make him uncomfortable, because his cheeks flush and he starts to turn back to the sink.

I reach for his arm, halting him mid-flight. "Hey. I'm sorry I was late. And drunk. That's not how I wanted our reunion to go down."

He shrugs, but doesn't look directly at me. "You had

a shitty day. It happens."

"But I didn't want it to. Not when I already owed you an apology for the Robbie thing."

Miller steps back out of my reach and rolls his eyes. "Forget about the Robbie thing."

I'm not sure I'll ever be able to forget Robbie the Fucknugget. Or his groping hands. That night was the catalyst for me. The thing that made me realize how far gone I actually was.

Getting him to admit his sins to Miller made me feel righteous. Punching him made me feel even better. I was protecting my best friend from a married, closeted jackass, after all, right? I was the hero.

And while Miller did kick him to the curb as soon as he found out the truth, he didn't exactly thank me or see me as his knight in shining armor.

"You were following him? Asking questions at his school? Why? Do you know how weird that is, Brendan? I'm a grown man and you're not my father. Who put you in charge of my virtue? You, of all people—the one who has sex with anyone alert enough to give their consent."

I tried to listen instead of acting like a damn deviant, but while he paced the room telling me off, I couldn't stop staring at the crack of his ass visible above his loose-fitting boxers. I was dizzy with how fast my dick had come to attention, and I knew in that moment I'd never reacted so violently, so passionately to anyone. But I didn't have an answer for why I'd been so determined to get dirt on his boyfriend.

I care about you, wouldn't have been enough. *You deserve better*, was true, but not what I really wanted to say.

Mine. It kept repeating in my head until I finally understood what it meant. It was a lot to grapple with. Too much. I didn't react to it as well as I should have.

"Someone needs to look after it. You nearly gave it away to that weaselly fucker, and you didn't even like him."

"I liked him enough to invite him over."

"Oh, I'm sorry. I thought you'd care that he was a cheater. I had no idea you were good with being a piece on the side."

"Of course I care! All I'm saying is I can deal with my relationships on my own."

"Relationships? You've never had a relationship. Have you ever even sucked a dick? You're wound so tight I'm surprised he got your shirt off."

I'm not going to lie. Things got progressively worse

after that, until Miller had enough and decided to kick me out as well.

I was pissed and frustrated, but even then I knew I'd crossed a line. And I'd done it because I couldn't face what I was feeling for him. Not at the time. And backwards as it sounds, I couldn't come back to make things right until I made sure I knew that it was real.

"Fine," I finally tell him. "We won't talk about it. But I'm sorry for hurting you. And for not coming back sooner."

He pats my arm and offers me a weak version of the pouty smile I love. "Let's start fresh this morning, okay? What happened before, everything that happened last night is just erased. Clean slate. Deal?"

I frown. He wants to erase everything that happened last night?

There's a tinge of panic in his expression that gives me my answer. I'm not sure how I feel about that but I won't push it. Yet. "Clean slate."

He beams in relief. "Great. Now go shower while I clean this kitchen before Royal gets here. The place is a mess."

It isn't. But Miller is a little OCD about keeping things clean. "Sounds good."

As I head up the stairs, I'm trying to decide how to approach things now that I'm back to square one with this clean slate idea of his. I know last night was a little out of control. Miller was surprised and unprepared. He never handles that well.

Aurelia once told me that Miller's need to control certain aspects of his life had to do with her illness. *"I've been all he's ever had. All he knows. He can't heal this thing inside me. He can't stop it. So what he can fix, what he can control, he must."*

His house. His job. His nice reliable Hyundai. The retirement savings account he started when he was seventeen. Miller Day is the most responsible, in-control thirty-year-old I know.

On the flip side, there's me. I never thought about the future, never had to consider saving for a rainy day and never had to worry about anything or anyone but myself.

Until Miller.

Him, I worry about. I never stop. I want things for him I'd never consider for myself, and most importantly, I want to be the one to give those things to him.

So if he needs control, or needs to go slow, I'll do the best I can to accommodate him. As long as I get to be there when he's finally ready to let go.

Miller Day is mine.

That's why I never trusted Robbie. Why I never liked the idea of Miller's neighbors setting him up while I was gone. It's why, no matter how far away I fly, I keep coming back home.

Now I've just got to convince Miller that I not only want him after a lifetime of playing for the other team, but I want the whole ballgame. Home, family…and apparently a dog.

I have to prove to him I can be trusted with his heart.

Tall order, I know.

CHAPTER FOUR

His Big, Hard Hammer

"Gripping hammers, nailing wood… I had no idea carpentry was so phallic, did you?" Royal asks, staring at the large metal nail gun in his fist.

My hammer slips, missing the nail and leaving a small chip in the cedar plank that I'm praying Miller doesn't see when he gets back from the vet with the dog.

When I glare over at Royal, he grins. "See, Brendan—that's why Miller gave *me* the nail gun and you got the hammer. Your aim sucks."

"Thanks for clearing that up. Would it make you happy if I nailed my thumb to the damn deck?"

Royal rolls his shoulders, his snug t-shirt straining against his large frame. "You think I'm still upset about last night? I'm not. Let it go, man. That's *my* theme song. Anyway, Austen's giving all of us a chance to make it up to her tomorrow. A do-over, she says. I was just making a simple observation."

And I'm still thinking about my dick. Which instantly makes me wonder what's taking Miller so long. "Yeah, okay. A do-over?"

Royal points his nail gun somewhat menacingly in my direction. "Your answer is *yes*. Whatever it is, you're going. You owe me that."

I know I do. And I don't care if she wants us to get pedicures, test out some of her famous facial scrubs or go skydiving in the buff. Royal has always been there for me, so I can take one for the team. "We'll be there."

He gives me a sideways glance. "We? So you and Miller are good now? All made up and friends again?"

"Yeah. We're good."

Only I want more than friendship and I'm not sure how to make that happen.

I thought about talking to him about that clean slate again, but by the time I got out of the shower, Miller was outside with Royal, walking him through hanging the floor joists in the frame he'd already built for the deck. I couldn't help but laugh as I watched Miller hand Royal the nail gun. The big Samoan held the foreign tool by its air hose, dangling it in front of him like a dead snake.

"So *this* is what a nail gun looks like."

I watched as Miller gently took the dangerous implement back, turned it up right and stuck into Royal's big palm.

"Maybe..." He looked around like he was searching for something, "...maybe we should practice on that first?" he suggested, pointing to something out of my line of sight. Probably a piece of scrap wood.

"Like this?"

I heard the distinctive *snap/hiss* of the nail gun firing a nail into wood.

"Wahoo! Holy crap, this is awesome!"

Snap! Snap!

"Yeah, kill that bad board, big guy," Miller chuckled, causing me to snort the water I'd been drinking up my nose.

I'm glad they get along so well. Miller deserves to have a big group of people who care about him. A family.

Royal sets down his new favorite toy and crosses his arms, whistling until he gets my attention.

"What's wrong?"

"Oh I'm just fine. Great really. But what's up with you, Buttercup?"

I waggle my eyebrows. "I was thinking about how adorable you look with that nail gun, sweetheart."

"How could you not? But seriously, tell me. My brother gives advice for a living. It's in my blood."

Raising one eyebrow, I line up another plank to nail down. "You aren't blood relatives."

"Tell me."

This will be my first test. Royal is openminded, his brother is gay and he's an all-around decent guy. On the other hand, we've picked up women together. Countless women. He knows more about my appetites than Miller would want to.

How will he react to my late-in-life change of heart?

I open my mouth and Royal holds up his hand. "Wait. Don't say it. No way."

"What?"

"No. Way."

I scowl. "I'm not starting this with you. Just tell me."

Royal grins at my irritation. "Was Austen right, buddy? Is the legendary Brendan Kinkaid now down for the D?"

"How would she know? And who even says that? It's

dick, not D. Use your damn words."

But he's too busy studying my guilty expression to worry about words. He lets out a loud whoop, grabbing me around the waist and lifting me off my feet like a rag doll. It feels like a bear attack. Or how I imagine a bear attack would feel if it was in an unusually affectionate mood.

"Put me down, lunatic. What's gotten into you?"

Not that he hasn't done this before, but it's usually reserved for when his team wins the Superbowl or he gets lucky in Iceland.

Royal sets me down, the bright smile taking up miles of his face. "Just being supportive, brother. Am I the first person you've come out to? I mean, other than Miller. I'm honored."

I take a step back, glancing toward the empty house and the next-door neighbors' windows. "Keep it down, I'm not coming out."

"No D?" Does Royal look disappointed?

I sigh. "Fine, yes, but I'm only into one and he doesn't know about it yet."

He might suspect something after last night. No wait. He's erased it on his stupid slate.

At least he seemed to be trying like hell to pretend it

never happened.

"We haven't been alone long enough for us to talk, but I'm working up to it." Confessing is easier than I thought it was going to be. It feels good to say it out loud. It feels right.

It feels—"What are you doing?"

Royal has his phone out, his wide thumbs flying across the screen.

"Texting my brother for you. Luckily, he and Carter were invited to a Finn thing this weekend. I hope he doesn't drive them too crazy with his new book idea. He keeps saying he wants to do a study on their family, all very scientific, of course. His husband doesn't think they'll appreciate it."

"What does that have to do with me?"

Royal winks at me. "His study? It seems an unusually high percentage of the men in that family like the D. I know, I know, use my words. They like dick. Penis. Anal. Cock and balls. Happy now?"

"Overjoyed."

"Anyway, between my brother and that crowd, someone should have some good advice on how to woo a guy in two weeks."

I'm not sure whether my heart is racing out of insult

or panic. "So when I said keep it down, what you actually heard was 'start a newsletter and tell everyone'? And since when do I need help?"

He slips his phone in his back pocket and shakes his head sadly. "You don't know."

"Know what, smartass?"

"How to romance. You've never actually done it. For years you've glided by on that rich-boy-wants-to-be-bad, kinky-Peter Pan charm of yours. But that only attracts the kind of woman who wants one night of dirty sex before she settles down with the boy next door."

"Wow, man. I think that drew blood. But don't sugarcoat it to spare my feelings." I turn and sit down heavily on the wooden steps that still need to be attached.

Royal drops his chin to his chest and sighs. "Look, *I* know you're a great guy. But that's not what you show to the women trying to get in your cockpit. Things have been pretty easy for you in the getting laid department, but in all the years we've known each other, you never hinted at wanting more."

I could say neither has he, but that wouldn't be true. Royal has always had as much, if not more, success with women than I have, but he never hid that he was open to falling in love. Even actively searching for it. He's just one of those guys who screams future soccer dad. He was built to have a family.

I was born to be a commodity, and I guess I've always acted accordingly.

"Do you think this is a bad idea?" That I'm not good enough for Miller because of my past?

Royal frowns. "Hell no, it's a great idea. It kind of makes sense, now that I think about it. He's the only one you've ever talked about on a regular basis. But the fact is, you have a track record that wouldn't look so hot on paper, and Miller is the opposite of what you used to call your type. He isn't female, he isn't easy, and unless I'm mistaken, you'd actually like to keep him."

When I nod, he says, "Good. So I did the right thing with the SOS text, because you'll need all the help you can get."

He doesn't know the half of it. "Miller's never…"

The loose stairs jostle and I'm forced to slide over to the edge as Royal sits down beside me. "Never? As in…*never?* Didn't he have a boyfriend the last time you were in town?"

"That fight I told you about? That was me clocking the lying little shit and making sure things never got that far."

"Damn, son. So that's what all that cockblock rambling was about last night. I knew Miller was a bit of homebody but… You've got your hands full, don't you?"

"Yep." I tilt my head in his direction. "So do you, by the way."

"You mean Austen?" Royal rubs his hands down his thick thighs and nods soberly. "I'm aware. I think the Waynes might be the biggest hurdle. I'm used to big families, but Matilda has always let us do our own thing—unless it infringed on someone else's rights or hurt the environment, you know? Hers…"

I pat his back supportively. "Well, *I* think they'll love you, but you shouldn't be wasting JD on me, man. He's right there in the belly of the beast. Austen has a brother *and* a sister who married into that Finn family right? Tell JD to put in a good word for *you*."

Royal snorts. "You think I'm giving him that kind of ammunition after all the grief I've given him over the years?"

"You haven't told him about Austen? What does he think you're doing in town?"

"Saving you from yourself." Royal smirks when I try

to push him off the steps. The man is as immovable as a mountain. "What? It isn't a lie. Especially now that I know how you'll be spending your surprise time off. You ready to tell me about that yet?"

"No."

"Fine. I'll find out eventually. Until then, think of me as that cricket on your shoulder."

"Big damn cricket," I mutter, making him laugh.

"Yes I am. And connected via text to an entire colony of gay or gay-adjacent crickets who can guide you through the perils of loving a socially awkward man-virgin with impressive carpentry skills and nosy neighbors."

As if on cue, an old Madonna song starts to blast out of Diane and Heather's open windows, making me think someone heard at least part of our conversation.

Like a Virgin.

"Jesus." I laugh and rub my hand over my face. "Why am I doing this to myself? Why are *you*? Remember when we had no one to answer to? When our biggest and only concern was what exciting destination we would fly to next?"

Royal's dark eyes sparkle as he stands and tugs me to my feet, slapping my hammer back into my hand.

"Everybody needs a direction, Kinkaid. And a solid place to land. Now let's get some of this work done so we can impress your future husband. From what I can tell, Day takes this shit seriously."

***

"Rub it, Miller. Please. Oh God. *Deeper*."

"If I go any deeper I'll— Yeah, that's a big one."

I wish this was as hot as it sounded. But despite the pain radiating from my neck to the middle of my back, I'm still turned on enough to be poking a hole in his mattress with my erection.

As long as I don't roll over, we should be good.

Fuck, I really want to roll over.

I don't think this was what Royal had in mind when he thought we could impress Miller with my handy skills. I'm not a moron. I have mastered the tech manuals of every bird I've ever flown and can do some pretty fancy math in my head. I understand the ins and outs of finance, thanks to the lectures that passed for dinner conversation in my childhood home. And I've been told I'm gifted with my tongue.

But I am unquestionably subpar when it comes to the fine art of backyard deck building.

Wasn't I the one who helped start the first three projects on this house?

Yes, you were, man with fragile ego. And you steamed off that ugly wallpaper like an Alpha dog champ. Feel better now?

"Oh God, right there," I moan when Miller digs into one particularly stubborn knot with his fingers of steel. Who has fingers that strong?

The massage therapist you want to nail.

Miller shifts closer. I feel his hips against mine as he hovers over my back to apply more pressure. "This is my fault. I shouldn't have left you two alone to go to the vet. I mean, it's a good thing I did, since Dix needed new heartworm medication, but I shouldn't have let you work on the deck while you were still hung over."

When a man talks about heartworms and you still want to fuck him? That's got to be love.

"I was fine."

Miller scoffed. "Obviously. Your neck's been hurting since you woke up, hasn't it? And you let Royal egg you on. He doesn't know his own strength."

Oh, Royal knows his own strength. He just doesn't realize that *I'm* only human, with a fragile back that's many, many years older than his.

Not that many.

"I had to do it," I grunt. "He was making me look bad, carrying all those planks over his shoulder."

"Royal would make the Hulk look bad, and he'd probably whistle a happy tune while he was doing it. You, on the other hand, should know better."

"What about our years of friendship tells you I should know better?"

But I really should. I just couldn't help myself. I heard Miller pull into the driveway, glanced over at my shirtless, Bunyan-esque buddy and felt the need to step up my game.

Dropping my sweat-soaked shirt on the ground, I reached for the next slab of cedar and imagined Miller looking through the window. He'd see me and not be able to look away. Maybe he'd slip his hand under those easy access sweatpants of his and stroke himself while I worked to build him a deck I could fuck him on.

That fantasy was abruptly cut short when the crick in my neck morphed into the kind of immobilizing pain that would have made a lesser man cry.

No one saw me cry, so it didn't happen.

"There," Miller grunts while I feel a firm, painful pressure.

A sudden rush of release, almost euphoria, hits me and I moan out loud. "Yes. Oh, thank God. Damn, I swear your hands should be bronzed for this."

He chuckles. "Sure, but if they were, they wouldn't be able to help you when this happens again. And we're not done yet."

We're not? Somebody up there loves me.

"I still need to…" One minute Miller is muttering to himself, and the next he's sitting on my ass, thighs gripping my hips as he works through the last of the knots in my back.

That causes a whole new kind of pain. But I would suffer through it forever if it means he stays right where he is. "Don't stop. I'll die if you stop."

"If I keep this up too much longer, I'll do more harm than good. You'll need to ice the area later and take a nice long shower. If it's still hurting tomorrow, I'll give you another rub down."

I know exactly where I want him to rub me next.

"Mmmhmmm." I groan my assent, every bit of concentration focused on the delicious weight settled on my ass. My hips pump against the bed to relieve the ache. Just once.

Twice.

I'm trying to be subtle, but when the hands on my back go suddenly still, I know I haven't succeeded.

"What—we should stop here."

"Please don't." I reach back and clasp his calf with my hand. "I'm not ready for you to stop yet."

Don't leave.

Miller lays his palms flat on my back, keeping them still, but not removing them completely. "I really don't think more would be a good idea."

"Yeah? Well, I don't think clean slates are that smart either."

Shit. I said that out loud.

I move then, turning until he falls onto the bed beside me, and then my dick is pressed between his spread thighs, my hands cupping his face. "Why don't you want to talk about what I did to you last night, Miller?"

The dusting of freckles on his cheeks stands out as he pales. I want to kiss every damn one. "You were drunk. You don't remember."

I skim his lips with my thumb. "I remember every second. I've been reliving it all day."

Miller blinks, a deep furrow appearing between his brows. "You're not—you don't—"

Frustrated and impatient, I yank down his sweatpants

so forcefully he bounces back on the bed, and then my hands are on him again. Silky skin, hard as I remembered and all mine. "I am. I do."

"Oh fuck," Miller moans, closing his eyes.

"Look at me," I demand. "I'm sober and I'm here and I want you to see me."

He refuses and I push down the shorts I was working in, sliding my cock against his and groaning at how good it feels. "This is how much I want you."

Eyes wide and dilated are suddenly gazing up into my face with wonder and a touch of trepidation. I wrap my hand around both our cocks and stroke them together, watching his spine arch, hips rocking against mine in reaction.

"Brendan!" he cries shakily. "Oh God that feels so..."

"We're not erasing this," I promise grimly, desperate to hold back long enough for him to find his release. "I'm not going to let you forget how fucking perfect this feels."

His head is shaking back and forth, hands fisting on the bed beside him as I fuck us both with my fist. He's the sexiest thing I've ever seen. And knowing I'm the one giving him pleasure makes me harder than I knew I could be.

"You like that?"

"Yes," he gasps, his feet planted on the mattress on either side of me as he lifts his hips with every stroke. "*Yes*."

"That's right," I growl, my hand pumping rough and fast up our slippery shafts. "This is how it's going to be when I fuck you, Millie. You'll be tighter than this fist when I finally get inside you."

He shouts his release and I tumble over the edge with him, his name on my lips. I'm rocked by the speed and force of my climax, the sight of my come on Miller's body only making it more intense.

It isn't until I come back down to earth that I realize something's wrong. "Miller?"

He slips out from underneath me, turning his back to tug up his pants. I sit up in concern. "Miller, talk to me."

"Can we not?" His voice is soft and a little distant. "I mean, we need to, but can it wait? Fred's coming over for dinner tonight and I need to clean up and check the deck and—"

I reach for his arm and he flinches. *Fuck*. "Shit, Miller. Did I screw up here?"

"It's new. I wasn't expecting…but we're good. I swear we're good. I just want to talk about it later."

I don't know what to do, but since I've made a mess of things again, I don't see another option. "Whatever you want. Just don't shut me out, okay?"

He nods and moves away, stopping at the bedroom door. "Don't forget the ice after your shower. I'll see you at dinner."

Royal is right. I can fuck, but I have no idea what I'm doing in the romance department.

Why did I push him so hard when I knew he had no experience?

You weren't thinking. You were feeling.

Feeling selfish.

Now I feel like an ass, and all I can think about it how much easier it would have been to keep that slate clean for a little while longer.

But there's no going back now and I don't want to. I just need to come at this in a different way. A different, less aggressive way that doesn't send him running again.

Here's hoping he gives me the chance.

CHAPTER FIVE

Sixty-Minute Man

Miller

Help!

I'm trapped in a locked room and this weekend is trying to kill me.

At the very least it might end up giving me a stroke. A man can only take so many shocks to his system before that system decides everything is crazy and upside down and a reboot might be the only way to straighten that shit out.

Let's recap while everyone's distracted with their Revolutionary War-based Escape Room puzzles, shall we?

I went out to a pub to get Austen and Royal together. That might have been my first mistake. I didn't think it through. Putting two outgoing, irritatingly cheerful and unceasingly energetic people in the same room to meet, possibly date and potentially fall in love is something I should have considered more carefully.

I mean, it's working, but I'm not sure it's a good thing. Individually they're a force of nature. As a team they might be unstoppable.

As if that's not enough, my straight friend—drunk at the time—gave me the best orgasm of my life before passing out. I'm a grown man so I handled it, but then he followed it up with a sneak attack the next day while I was helping him recover from a neck injury, blowing my mind again.

"This is how it's going to be when I fuck you."

I know I said earlier my life was not a porno, but maybe I spoke too soon because *who says something like that*?

Brendan Kinkaid.

And I'll be damned if his words didn't turn me into some kind of sex-starved animal mid-mating-season.

I admit, I was already turned on from that massage. I felt bad that he'd hurt himself while working on my deck, but I wasn't mad that it had given me an excuse to touch him.

I wasn't expecting him to like it that much. I definitely wasn't expecting him to tell me that he wanted to talk about what happened the night before. That he not only remembered it, but he wanted a repeat.

Twice. It's happened twice.

The first time, he fell asleep. The second time? He stayed away and I ran like a scared little virgin on his wedding night.

It's embarrassing, but we all know that's exactly what I did.

I'm used to his flirty banter and ass slapping. Used to wanting to touch him every time he's in the room while he remains oblivious. But the focus of this highly sexual man directed at me? Wanting me?

I wasn't ready for that, no matter how many times I've imagined it.

So yes, I used Fred and the dog and the deck to avoid being alone with him for the rest of the evening. Yes, I went to bed and spent the entire night trying to resist jerking off to the memory of what he'd done to me hours before.

Note, I said *trying*.

And yes, I agreed to the Austen do-over date because I'd promised her, and I thought it would give me a little more time to think. To keep my distance.

I didn't know my dear friend would trap the four of us in a tiny fucking room filled with riddles and padlocks with nothing to do for an entire hour but work in close proximity if we wanted to escape this room.

An escape room. Is an actual room people pay to be locked into. For *fun*.

I did *not* see that coming, it was the last thing I expected her to choose, and I absolutely want to escape it.

Austen nudges me and I realize I've been staring at a painting of Benjamin Franklin playing some instrument made of glass bowls while I had my silent nervous breakdown.

"Do you see a clue or are you avoiding us?" she asks.

That second thing.

"Well…" I scramble to explain my reasons for impersonating a statue. "We're supposed to be figuring out some code Franklin created to hide the location of his secret weapon against the British right? To win the war?"

She leans against me with a soft laugh. "Yes. But I

don't think he won anything with his glass armonica. It might have been his favorite but it never really took off. I suppose it could be used as a weapon, though. Especially if the British had unusually sensitive eardrums."

I give her some side eye. "Know-it-all, Sherlock."

"Daughter of a professor, my dear Watson. We own a lot of books on good old Ben."

She gestures furtively behind me and I glance over my shoulder. Royal and Brendan are on the opposite side of the room, arguing quietly over a cypher for a combination lock as if the safety of the country is at stake.

Which *is* the basic gist of this scenario, and I almost feel unpatriotic for not helping. It's just…odd. They look like they're having a blast.

"Something happened between you two, didn't it?" she whispers, reaching out to feel the edges of the picture frame for clues while she's talking, because she's a badass multi-tasker who wants to kick some Redcoat tail.

"Stop doing that," I hiss back, picking up a book at random and leafing through the pages.

"Doing what?"

"Reading my mind."

"So I'm right?" she asks with innocent delight.

"You know you are. But *I* still don't know what it means or what to do about it."

That's the only puzzle I'm desperate to solve.

Brendan Kinkaid is straight. I've seen him with women. A lot of women. And I've heard stories of his and Royal's conquests for years, whether I wanted to or not.

I also know he has never, in all the time I've known him, kissed me or touched me or said anything that would lead me to believe he was bi until this weekend.

Trouble at work and losing his condo could explain some of his strange behavior, but not all of it.

"This is how it's going to be when I fuck you."

I think I'm just having a hard time believing this is real.

"Royal thinks he's into you."

A piece of paper flutters to the floor and we both kneel down to pick it up while continuing our hushed conversation. "Royal is crazy. I'm glad you found out now before I get an invitation to the wedding."

She blushes and I forget about my own problems long enough to tease her. "I take it this setup is working out for you?"

She gives me a short but vehement nod in answer. "And he's wearing *shorts*, Miller. It's like he knows that sexy calves are my weakness."

I almost burst out laughing, but manage to restrain myself. "He didn't hear it from me."

Maybe Royal's a witch too.

"They're just so damn defined." She fans herself and throws me a wink. "And he's funny. You never see a hot-and-funny combo anymore. Not Irish, but I can definitely work with that."

I look at the paper and frown. "I think this might be important."

"You and Brendan are what's really import— Wait, let me see that." She snatches it out of my hands and gets to her feet.

"Lost time is never found again," she reads out loud, her voice raised for Royal and Brendan to hear. "I think that's from Poor Richard's Almanack."

Royal, who's managed to open up the locked box while we were talking about his calves, holds up a timepiece that's dangling from a chain. "I found it."

"I *almost* found it," Brendan said defensively, but he was smiling, clearly enjoying himself. "I definitely solved the key puzzle that got us the cypher. And it's a good thing Diane wasn't here or we'd still be on that crossword."

"Hey." I feel the need to defend my neighbor, despite the fact that she really is just pathetically bad at crossword puzzles.

"Yes, you've solved everything, brother." Royal rolls his eyes in our direction as he soothes Brendan's ego. "We'll buy you a trophy once our sixty minutes are up."

I hang back as the trio gathers around the watch, turning it over and studying every knob and design etched on the gold casing in search of the next clue.

I don't trust myself that close to Brendan yet.

Don't judge me.

"This reminds me of that Nicholas Cage movie," Brendan says in hushed excitement.

"Gone in Sixty Seconds?" Royal asks absently, running his fingers over the face.

"That's about stealing cars. The other one."

"Con Air?"

Austen chuckles. "A plane full of criminals that's basically a poor man's remake of Die Hard? Sure. That's exactly what this is like."

Royal looks momentarily dazzled. "I knew you'd like

Die Hard."

Brendan made a sound of frustration. "No, it's the other one. He's—"

"National Treasure," I say a little louder than I intended, because honestly this could take all night.

"Yes," Royal and Brendan shout simultaneously, sending me matching looks of gratitude and pointing like I just scored a touchdown.

Austen smiles up at Royal "I didn't realize you were such a movie buff."

"We're not," Brendan answers for him. "But you'd be surprised how many Nicholas Cage movies play on international flights. There's no escaping it. Kind of like this room."

I'm the one who figured it out, but saying that out loud would ruin their moment and draw too much attention my way. Besides, I think wandering around to keep Brendan at a distance has had some advantages. Like discovering our ticket out of here. "Hey Austen? What time does that watch have?"

"One seventeen exactly," Austen says, joining me beside the bookcase I'm studying. "Why?"

There's a mantel clock on the center shelf. It's topped with a small bronze figure of Benjamin Franklin, and the glass covering is lying beside it, almost like an invitation. Taking a chance, I move the hands to one-seventeen and we all hear a loud, whirring click before the bookshelf opens to reveal a hidden room.

"You did it!" Austen hugs me quickly and then she's racing around me to explore the new area.

Not the way out then. Just *another locked room.*

Help?

Royal ducks his head beneath the smaller door to follow her, and before I can join them, Brendan's arms slip around me, pulling me back against his chest. "Are you ever going to talk to me again?"

Not if I can help it, I want to shout, but I know that's unrealistic and childish. "I'm talking to you now."

"Miller."

I sigh. "Of course I am. But maybe now is not the right time for this particular topic?"

"They're playing with electricity," he murmurs against my temple. "And it's never going to be the right time if you keep avoiding me."

I lean back, my body reacting to his nearness the way I knew it would. I never realized how hungry I was for this kind of affection. "I'm not avoiding you."

His laugh is like a dirty secret in my ear. "Liar. Ever

since I jumped you in the bedroom, you've been giving me the silent treatment." He hesitates. "If I stepped over the line and you want me to leave the house, just tell me. I'll never make you do something you're not comfortable with. I hope that you know that."

"No." I turn around in his arms and tug him away from the open door. "I mean, yes I know that, and I don't want you to leave. But can you blame me for freaking out? You show up after months of no contact and start acting like—like you—"

"Like I want you?" Brendan's dark eyes glitter as they stare down at my lips. "It's not an act, Miller. The question I stupidly thought I knew the answer to is, do *you* want *me*?"

Don't answer that. It's a trap.

My fingers are digging into his hips, but I'm not sure if it's to pull him closer or keep him at a safe distance. "Six years, Brendan. You've never wanted me before. Something like that doesn't change overnight."

A dark thought crosses my mind and every muscle in my body tightens, preparing for a blow or the wrong answer. "This isn't about the Robbie thing again, is it? Do you feel so bad about me not getting laid that you're trying to make up for it? Because that would be seriously fucked up."

I know I'm wrong the instant the surprise in his expression turns to anger. He walks me back into the wall and reaches for my hand, forcing it between us to cup him through his jeans.

Despite my surprise, my hand instinctively flexes around the hard, hot length of him and he grits his teeth, leaning into my touch.

"If you're trying to piss me off, it's working," he rasps. "I may not be going about this the right way—the slow, methodical, romantic way—but I refuse to believe you don't know me well enough to realize the last thing I'm thinking about when I'm touching you is that asshole who didn't deserve to breathe your air."

The possessiveness in his gaze makes me gasp. "Then why are you doing this?"

"Isn't wanting you this much enough?" He lowers his head to bite down gently on my chin. "Tell me I'm not wrong. Tell me you want me back."

"You know I do."

He breathes out a sigh of relief that makes me shiver. "We can be so good together, Millie. I can show you. I just need to get you alone and willing for a long enough period of time to prove it to you."

Sex. He wants sex.

Fuck, who am I kidding? So do I.

Why shouldn't it be him? You've wanted him for years. It's not like you're holding out for marriage.

What about our friendship? This could ruin it. He could remember he's not remotely gay and fly away for good.

And that would be different from the last few months, how? At least this time, you'd have a happy memory to remember him by. You'd know what it felt like to be with him. To be with someone you wanted.

A part of me still thinks this is a cry for help, and that if I were a better friend I would back him down off this ledge and help him work through whatever it is that's causing him to act so out of character. But I'm having a hard time being that better friend right now.

Maybe it's all the blood rushing to my dick that's making me think this is a good idea. But the truth is, if he wants me, there's no way I'll be able to resist him, and right now only the scared, virginal control freak inside me wants to try.

Fuck that guy.

"Alone and willing?" I pant as he kisses his way up my neck. "I think we can make that happen if we ever get out of this room."

The fingers wrapped around my wrist tighten at my response and he lifts his head. He's looking in my eyes like I have answers there, but I know I don't. I'm not sure of anything right now. This could be the craziest decision I've ever made, but if he really wants me, I'll have to risk it.

A knock on the bookshelf startles us both and I drop my hand from his dick, turning my head to see a wide-eyed Austen waiting to be noticed. "So," she starts hesitantly. "The monitor on the wall wants to talk to you."

I frown in confusion until Brendan takes my chin and guides my head around to face the television screen on the far wall, which is supposed to show us clues if we need them.

There are cameras everywhere.
We can see and hear you.
Cut it out.
Fifteen minutes left.

I'm not embarrassed. I'm never coming here again and I'll run the other way if I see anyone who works here on the street…but I'm not embarrassed.

"Thanks, Austen," I mumble, face boiling.

Royal leans around the corner, his head over Austen's shoulder and traces of her burgundy lipstick staining his lips. "Big brother wanted to talk to us too," he says with a mischievous grin, chuckling when she whacks him in the stomach.

"What? It's true. Let's quit wasting time and go save our nation."

It's nearly impossible for us to concentrate after that. There isn't a lot of puzzle solving, but there is a lot of laughing, touching and innuendo all around. When we get to the three-minute mark, we finally cave and ask for help.

I never did find out what Franklin's weapon was, but when the door finally opens we all cheer like we won the war.

If it were up to me, I'd run out that door and go straight home, dragging Brendan behind me, but Austen included lunch at the sandwich shop as part of the do-over date of awesome.

I'm a good friend. A *very* good friend who might die as the first successful gay virgin Cupid with blue balls if she doesn't let us leave soon.

I can tell when she looks at me she understands my dilemma. Which is why I also think this is her way of making sure I'm thinking straight, and that this is really what I want. Especially when she starts giving Brendan her gentle version of the third degree halfway through lunch.

"So what's this incident I keep hearing about? The reason you got suspended and drunk and almost ditched us at the pub?"

Yep. That's her gentle version.

Brendan puts down his half-eaten sandwich and reaches for a napkin, looking distinctly uncomfortable.

My instant thought is, *I really want to get laid, so I hope this doesn't have anything to do with sex at inappropriate elevations.*

"It was nothing," he demurs, making Austen raise her eyebrows.

Shit. She's got that look again.

"Really? It didn't seem like nothing Friday night."

Brendan shifts in his seat and I put my hand on his thigh beneath the table, offering support. The desire that was lurking under the surface ignites in his eyes and I know work is the last thing he wants to talk about.

Join the club.

"Captain Kinkaid was a real American hero," Royal says. "And he was drunk because people kept wanting to toast him for it. I should know. I got an email last night with a link to the video."

"Son of a bitch," Brendan mutters. "Who sent it?"

The big man shrugs as he takes out his phone. "I know people."

They stare at each other across the table, having a silent conversation that I'm absolutely convinced goes something like this:

Don't do it.

Oh, I'm doing it.

I'm warning you.

Doing. It.

My mom used to say that as a language, Guy was fairly easy to translate.

"Royal, give B a break," I say. "You know he's had a tough couple of days."

Brendan glances at me in surprise, his hand covering mine where it still rests on his thigh. *Because I can't stop touching him.*

Royal shakes his head. "I promise it's not bad, Miller. Brendan doesn't want to toot his own horn, but it might give Austen a few of those answers she's looking for."

He turns the screen of his smartphone toward the

three of us and presses play.

I lean forward to watch a man with a beer gut and an abrasive attitude heckle the woman across from him on the plane. She's half his size and she reminds me a little of my mother, just watching him rant with a serene expression on her face. Like his words aren't horrifying her.

She tries to reassure him that she's simply a passenger, not a terrorist, but her compassion has the opposite effect, working him into a red-faced frenzy. He gets to his feet, and at that point I think he's on something. He's not making any sense. I can make out that he wants the rest of the passengers to help him take her down, but the instant he reaches for her, he's on the ground with two men gently but firmly restraining his flailing limbs.

"That's Doug, the air marshal," Brendan mutters in my ear. "He had one of the flight attendants grab me in case he needed backup."

I'm not seeing anything wrong with this. It happens, right? Crazy people get airline tickets all the time, and no one is being physically harmed. There's nothing on here that would get him suspended. "But why—"

"Just watch," Royal says, shushing me with a hand

gesture.

They finally get the man back in his seat and he's nodding as if letting them know he's in his right mind, but just when Brendan turns to walk back to the cockpit, the jackhole gets to his feet again and decides to accuse him of not standing up for Americans.

Apparently that was the wrong thing to say.

Brendan is suddenly every hero of every war movie I've ever seen. Even the ones with aliens. Whoever made the video put sweeping orchestra music behind it, which was genius, because, while I can't hear everything he's saying, I know it's the best, most patriotic speech I've heard in my life.

Basically, he let the whole plane know that the woman under attack was more American than the idiot who questioned her based on his own ignorant assumptions.

When beer gut tried to hit him for calling him ignorant, Brendan knocked him out cold with one punch, at which point he received a standing ovation from the rest of the passengers.

I wince.

That's why he got suspended for two weeks.

"I shouldn't have done that," he mumbles. "I knew

better."

Screw that. I want this hero to fuck me. Now.

"We need to go," I say abruptly, pushing back my chair and getting to my feet. "Thanks for the…yeah. We should go."

Royal covers his mouth to hide what I know is a shit-eating grin, but Austen just looks over at Brendan with her all-seeing, perfectly made up eyes before holding out her hand. "I approve."

Well, thank baby Jesus for that.

Brendan shakes her hand with a smile and then gets up to stand beside me, his palm firm and hot on my back. "I'll talk to you later Royal. And by later, I mean tomorrow afternoon at the earliest."

I think everyone at this table knows what later means.

Even the virgin.

Chapter Six

Ready or Not

I let Brendan drive so I can send out an emergency text to Fred and Heather.

Me: *Will someone dog-sit Dix? And then stay away from the house until you hear from me. Thanx*

Heather: *Does this mean what I think it means?! Brendan? I knew it!*

Fred: *Well, I'm too young to know it. I'll take Dix.*

Me: *I owe you.*

Fred: *There's a march next Saturday.*

Me: *I was thinking pie or pocket change.*

Fred: *You owe me liberty or death.*

Me: *Fine. Liberty.*

Heather: *Don't worry. I'll distract Diane and hide the binoculars.*

Fred: *You have binoculars?*

Heather: *Yes, dear. We used them before the dinosaurs invented hidden cameras to watch our neighbors do the horizontal mambo.*

Me: *We're all too young to know that. Talk tomorrow.*

I set down the phone and notice Brendan's white-knuckled grip on the steering wheel. My heart stutters. "Change your mind?"

He reaches for my hand, placing it firmly on his thigh. "Its just nerves."

He's nervous? I've got thirty years' worth of inexperience that should be making me a wreck right now. What we've done together is more than anything I've—

"Flying I can do in my sleep, but I don't really drive that much anymore. It feels unnatural."

I laugh, and I'm not sure if it's relief or hysteria, but once I get started it's hard to stop. "*That's* what the nerves are about? *Driving*?"

He glances over at me, returning both hands to the

wheel. "What did you think it was about?"

"I'll give you one guess," I say, catching my breath and leaning back against the seat. But from his scowl he already knows.

"I may be impatient," he says gruffly. "But I'm not nervous. Not about being with you."

I like the way his rough admission makes me feel. Alive. Exciting. Since he came back to town, I've been more aware of myself, of my body, than I have in years. My emotions are more intense. It's overwhelming and new, but I can't help wanting more of what I've been missing.

And I've missed more than most.

It wasn't a conscious choice at first, but even before Mom got sick, she was struggling to raise me with no partner or family to give her a hand. It was the two of us against the world. I don't regret that, but it didn't leave much room for anyone else.

Everyone is lonely at some point in their lives. If it goes on long enough, it becomes normal. There's nothing to fix or make better if it's normal. It's life and you accept it, not knowing what you're missing.

I didn't know. Neither did Aurelia Day, who told me everything she knew about my father on the morning I got up the courage to ask who he was.

She didn't know much.

He was British, because his accent was the first thing that caught her attention. She liked his eyes. My eyes. He'd ordered tea instead of coffee at the diner where she'd worked, he never offered his number, even though she'd given him hers, and he'd disappeared the next morning with no idea that I was going to arrive nine months later.

It wasn't the great love story I'd been expecting, but my mother had no regrets about the outcome. She told me that from the moment she found out she was pregnant she knew everything happened for a reason. I was her reason.

"You're the only man I need, Millie."

I used to think I knew everything about her, but I don't know if she was ever in love or lust, or ever felt anything close to what I feel for Brendan. Unfortunately, I think I have a good idea what she'd say if she knew, because she was still alive when my crush on him grew obvious enough for her to notice.

"I love that boy, and he loves this family. He needs us, Millie. And you'll need him when I'm gone. Don't let a temporary feeling like desire get in the way of what

really matters."

I've always followed her advice. Believed it. It made sense, and what I feel for him never has. It also hasn't gone away. No matter where he goes, what he does or who he does it with, it's still there. And when he comes back, it's like he never left. Like I've been waiting.

Knowing Brendan like I do, this has to be a temporary thing. And temporary is something I've never been good with. I'm not a fan of uncertainty either. It's why working on the house is so satisfying for me. There's a plan I have control over, steps to take and a completed result that's solid and visible and real.

People aren't that simple. But since he told me he wants me, since he touched me? There's really no other decision to make. I don't want to let go of this feeling until I have to. Not even if the worst happens, and I lose him when it's over.

"What are you thinking about?"

I look out the window and I know where we are. There's a side street coming up that's narrow and overgrown and leads to a dead end. I've heard from my neighbors that people only go down this road for two reasons. Sure, most of those people are in high school, but I feel like a teenager right now—all hormones and no sense.

“I’m thinking you should turn left,” I say, squeezing his thigh.

Clearly confused, he follows my directions. “We’re five minutes away from the house, Miller. Do we need to stop somewhere?” He swears, shaking his head. “Supplies, right? You don’t have any—”

I laugh again, feeling lighter than I have in a while. “I have toothbrushes for random strangers, and you don’t think I’d be prepared for *that*? Stop the car.”

Unbuckling my seatbelt, I turn onto my knees and reach beneath the backseat for the bag I know I left there months ago.

“What the hell are you doing?”

“One of the stylists at Indulgence has a cousin who just got married. She brought me a goody bag from his bachelor party in the hopes that I would find someone to enjoy it with.”

She was doing it to be bitchy, but right now she’s my favorite person because everything I could ever need is inside. Flavored lube, condoms, a partially melted chocolate penis—

Okay, I forgot that was in there.

When I kneel back on my seat, going through the

bag, I notice him staring at me strangely. "Why did I stop here, Miller?"

"I'm impatient too. Too impatient to wait for everyone to get tired of looking out their windows so they can watch us walk up the drive. I wanted something first. Something I've never been brave enough to try before."

"What? Parking in broad daylight?" Brendan's teeth dig into his lower lip as he studies me. "Have you been hiding a wild streak of exhibitionism you haven't told me about?"

He makes me wild. "Do you want to find out?"

"More than you know."

That's all I needed to hear. I put my hand between his legs and reach under his seat, pushing it back to give us more room.

Brendan grabs me by my waist and positions me until I'm straddling his lap. "Two men in their thirties with a perfectly respectable bed, making out in the front seat of a car," he grumbles, holding me tighter when my back bumps the steering wheel. "We're taking a chance we could get interrupted again. Or pull a muscle."

I snort out a small laugh and push a button that has the seat reclining enough to give us more room. "I'll try and make it worth it, old man."

This time I'm the one kissing him, and the power of that is nearly as heady as his taste. He groans and relaxes beneath me, letting me take the lead.

I brush our lips together, touching his tongue with mine, teasing until he tilts his head to deepen the connection. Just like that first time, I'm instantly lost, unable to think about anything but how good he makes me feel.

The heat we're generating in the close space is making me sweat. So are the big thumbs that are rubbing hypnotically on my hips bones just beneath the waistband of my jeans. Back and forth…back and forth...until all I can think about is getting us both naked. I want to taste every inch of the man I've spent years dreaming about.

Why are we wasting time making out in my car?

Because I dreamed about this, too. Stolen moments that I missed by not dating in high school or going to prom or moving away for college. Those forbidden memories other people look back on with a glint in their eyes. Sweet, self-inflicted torture, when you're so crazy for each other you can't breathe, but you have to wait. Because you're too young, or your parents are home, or you promised not to go all the way until you were ready.

I'm a masochist. My unrequited crush on my best friend is now mutual, he's right here and ready to take me to bed, and I'm giving him a fully clothed lap dance while he makes deliciously pained noises and can't seem to stop biting and sucking on my upper lip.

"Please, Millie."

I reach blindly for the bottle of lube, wrapping his hand around it and grazing my lips over his ear. "I want your fingers inside me."

"Fuck," he says roughly, fumbling to flip the cap open. One strong hand reaches between us and rips open my jeans with a force that makes me moan in delight.

I grab the waist of my pants and shove them down a few inches until they stop at Brendan's thighs. My cock is trapped in my bunched-up underwear, but I'm too impatient to stop. I should have thought this through.

Just when I'm about to suggest we move to the back seat, he grabs the cheek of my ass and spreads it wide, using the lubed fingers of his other hand to trace the tight pucker that's clenching with arousal and anticipation.

"Are you sure you want to do this here?"

I suck on the skin of his neck, leaving a mark. "I need

it, Brendan."

He groans and pushes his finger inside, making me gasp.

"Tell me if it's too much."

"More," I moan, rocking back on his finger until it's fully inside me. "Another."

This time Brendan doesn't hesitate.

"*Oh God.*"

I've done this to myself but there's no comparison. His fingers are huge, two of them pulsing with shallow thrusts inside my ass. There's a pinch of pain, an impossible fullness and sparks lighting up every nerve in my body. Just from his fingers. I might combust when he finally gets his cock inside me. "That's good."

"You like that?" he asks hotly. "Having your tight little ass fingered by a man for the first time?"

"I love it."

He makes another pained sound, fingers curving and pumping deeper inside me. A third joins the mix, stretching me until I cry out in surprise. It's almost too much. I'm sucking in air and forcing myself to relax around him, but I can't get my bearings.

"You can take it," he rasps against my cheek. "I need you to take it so you're ready for more."

"I'm ready." I've been ready for years.

"Not for this." Brendan's thrusts pick up speed, hitting a spot that makes me shake and scream against his shoulder.

"Yeah, I know about that, and I'll be pushing that button all night, making you come so hard you cry. I need to make sure you can take what I need to give you. I don't want you walking away again until we're both satisfied."

"I won't," I swear hoarsely. "I'm not going anywhere."

His arm is a steel band around me, holding me close as his fingers thrust deeper, faster until I'm begging for release. "Please."

"Love you like this. I'm so fucking hard for you," he growls. "Come on my fingers so I can get you home and stretch this tight, virgin hole with my cock."

"Brendan!" Small explosions burst along my spine as the orgasm hits me. He swears when I tighten around his fingers but he doesn't stop, fucking me through every clenching pulse, drawing out the pleasure until I'm spent and shaking.

I didn't even touch myself, but my underwear has one hell of a wet spot. He did this to me. His dirty promises. His button-pushing.

"Shit."

I lift my head and see the strain on his handsome face. His brown eyes are nearly black, his cheeks flushed with feverish need.

Still trembling with aftershocks and hungry to return the favor, I scramble off his body and reach for his jeans.

"I need to get you home."

"You need to come, and I need to have another first."

"You want to suck my cock, Millie?"

More than you will ever know, I think as I tug his thick erection out of his pants. I've wanted him in my mouth for so long. "Lean back, Brendan."

He lowers the seat all the way now, lifting his ass to push his jeans down to his knees. No underwear to get in the way of this view—smart man—and when I finally get a good look, there's no doubt how badly he wants this.

"So big and thick," I say, stroking his shaft with the tips of my fingers and tracing every vein. When I get to the base, I run my fingers through the soft, dark hair that he keeps closely trimmed, cupping his tight balls lightly.

"I want these in my mouth," I murmur to myself.

"Do it. Whatever you want, as long as you don't

tease me."

When I lean in and lick the spot right beneath the head of his cock, it makes him wild. "I like teasing you."

Brendan cups my neck, squeezing a seductive warning. "Not this time. You can't promise me that pouty mouth of yours and not deliver. I want it wrapped around my cock. I want to watch those golden eyes fill with tears from trying to take me. I need your mouth on me, Millie."

He's looking at me like I'm the sexiest thing he's ever seen and the desire to tease him disappears.

"Show me how," I say softly.

His eyes flare with possessiveness. "Open your mouth for me, Miller."

He grabs a handful of my hair, guiding me closer until I wrap my lips around his cock, taking as much of him in my mouth as I can. My eyes nearly roll back from the taste. Why did I wait so long to do this?

You were waiting for him.

Musky man. Salt and heat. Brendan.

His strong thighs quiver beneath my palm, and I know I never want to forget this moment. Any of it. This is what I was waiting for.

His hips tilt up, driving his thick cock deeper, filling

my mouth and hitting the back of my throat. My eyes water and I look up at him, shivering at the satisfaction on his face. That hunger I never expected to see aimed in my direction.

"Look at you," he says, his tone guttural. "Outside, in broad daylight, taking your first cock. You want everyone to see how hard you make me? You want to send me over the edge?"

Yes.

I'm the one making him lose control now. I'm the one sucking him deep and making him beg. Brendan wants what I can give him. Needs it.

I cup his balls again, tugging until he gasps and his grip on my hair tightens until it's almost painful. Perfect.

"Harder," he says darkly. "Suck me harder and finish me off. Then I'll tie you to the damn bed and take my turn."

I let him go to press my hand against my hardening erection, desperate for what he's describing.

"No," he barks. "That's mine now. I'll give you all your firsts. I'll be the one who makes you come."

A whimper escapes my throat, and my desire for control starts slipping. I want to give it to him. I want him to take it from me.

I suck harder, relaxing my throat and reveling in his shout as I swallow around him. A part of me wants to laugh in delight that I can do this. That I am doing this. My first time. With Brendan. And it's so damn good.

"Fuck, Millie."

He's close. He loosens his grip in my hair, but I won't lift my head. I need to taste his release.

When he comes, the head of his cock swells in my mouth as he pumps his hips up toward my face. I feel his first salty gush as it pulses into my mouth and over my tongue. *Yes*.

My groan vibrates between us as I taste him for the first time. I tighten my lips to try to keep it all in, to swallow all of Brendan. Greedy for him. Craving more. Loving this.

Loving him.

I don't lift my mouth until I've cleaned his still-hard shaft, lapping at his stomach to get every drop.

"You like how I taste?"

I'm crazy for it.

"Mmmhmm."

Brendan is up on his elbows, watching me with a sultry, hooded gaze. "If you don't stop now, we're not going to make it home before I fuck you."

I'm tempted, more than I thought I could be, but I want what he's been promising even more.

Tied to my bed.

I sit up, licking my lips clean as he slips his cock back into his jeans with a grimace.

He stops, shaking his head as he studies me. "Jesus, you're so damn sexy. You have no idea, but you can't hide it anymore, Day. I hope you're ready for what comes next."

Ready or not.

I buckle my seatbelt with fingers that feel clumsy and thick. I did that. This was my idea.

The neighbors would be so proud.

When my street comes into view, I feel a momentary resurgence of my inner control freak.

Are you sure you want to do this? I know you're high on endorphins and feeling no pain, but there's no refund on this decision. Once you've lost it, you can't get it back.

If what we just did was what I've been missing out on? I don't fucking want it back. I want to lose it so thoroughly, I forget it ever existed.

I wonder if Brendan knows just how willing I am. He's quiet again, either focusing on the drive or thinking about what's going to happen as soon as we get behind closed doors.

"I want you to," I say into the silence.

He swerves slightly as he looks at me. "You want me to what?"

"Tie me to the bed."

"Damn it." His laugh comes out as a groan. "You can't say shit like that while I'm driving, Miller. We're one block away from the house and you're trying to make me wreck this car."

"I mean it." I turn toward him. "I'm giving you permission to tie me down."

He pulls into the driveway with a sigh of relief and turns off the engine, his eyes now fully on me. "Is this because of what I said? What you think *I* want? This is your first time, Miller. It should be what you want. Special."

I shake my head. "It should be whatever we want it to be. I'm not a teenager. I admit I'm late to the game, but I know what I can take."

Brendan looks like he wants to grab me and pick up where we left off, but then he looks out the car window and his face tightens. "Inside. Now."

"I have bungee cords in the garage," I say before I

get out of the car and walk swiftly toward the house. I have to bite my lip to stop smiling like a lunatic.

I deliberately avoid looking across the street or toward the windows next door. I don't even need to look over my shoulder to know I just made Brendan crazy.

Maybe I have been hiding a wild streak.

Who knew?

Chapter Seven

Burning Down the House

Brendan

Miller Day has hidden depths.

Not so hidden anymore.

I thought I knew him. All the small details, like the fact that he's not as awkward as he thinks in social situations, and he usually ends up gravitating toward the people who *are* and making them more comfortable. That he thrives on routine and keeping his hands busy, and he has the need to fix anything or anyone that's broken. That he's loyal, even when the person he's being loyal to doesn't always deserve it. And I know that I want him more than I've ever wanted anything in my life.

What I didn't know was that once he stopped holding back, I'd be the one knocked for a loop. I didn't know that those busy hands—that mouth—would destroy my restraint and make me so desperate to claim him that *my* hands would be the ones shaking. Or that this sudden embrace of his sexuality would make me feel as jittery as a damn virgin.

I had plans. I was going to go slow. Seduce him instead of scaring him away. With all the tricks I'd learned over the years and a few I'd read about but never tried, I was going to get him so addicted to my touch that he'd be willing to give me whatever I wanted.

How's that going for you?

My plan for the seduction of Miller Day was shredded in the front seat of his reliable Hyundai. He made me pull over, climbed on top of me and dared me to take what I wanted.

I'm giving you permission to tie me down.

Somehow the tables have turned and I'm the one being seduced. I'm not sure I'll survive the night.

I manage to get us back into the house without the neighborhood watch showing up to interrogate us, which is good because I can't concentrate on anything but the man beside me. The virgin who calmly told me where I could find a bungee cord.

Jesus, I need to get ahold of myself.

Miller is already upstairs. Waiting. His shirt is flung on the bottom step carelessly and I pick it up, knowing he wouldn't like finding it on the floor later.

What's happening to you, man? Next thing you know you'll be using coasters. Was the blowjob that good?

It was better.

When Miller decides to do something, there's no halfway about it. I should have known, and most of me is celebrating that fact with mental fireworks and parades, but there's another part of me that worries we might be going too fast.

I've fucked this up before. Taken more than he was ready to give. What if I do it again?

I walk through the kitchen to the garage door in a daze.

"Bungee cord," I mutter, reaching for my phone in desperation.

Me: *I need a cricket.*

Royal: *Big damn cricket at your service. Thought I wouldn't hear from you for a while.*

Me: *Desperado. Too soon?*

Royal and I have been with women all over the world, and they all have their own special kinks, so we created a code. Desperado means she likes rope and wants to be tied up, so I think he'll understand the question.

Royal: *I shouldn't know this. Should I know this?*

Me: *Probably not. Tell me anyway.*

Royal: *JD says if he asked for it, go to town.*

Me: *Even if...*

Royal: *I told him he was a control freak with no experience. He says it makes sense. It might relax him.*

Tying him up might relax him? I'm not sure if that's right, but I really fucking want it to be. JD is an advice columnist—that means I have to take his advice, right?

Tell me I'm right.

Me: *Roger that. Why aren't you with Austen, where I left you? Was that kiss the end of the date?*

There's a pause.

Royal: *This is JD. Thank you so much for the info. I have to make a few phone calls to everyone I know now.*

Me: *Shit. If you see this, Royal, I'm sorry.*

I turn off my phone, stuff it in my pocket and search for the bungee cord, cursing myself for ruining Royal's night.

Then I think about Miller and the roadside BJ again. Was that another way for him to control the situation? So he could have what he wanted, take a test run on his desires without being able to go too far?

We went far enough to make me insane, I think wryly as I find the bundle of bungee cords and work one free, testing the give. This will do for his first time.

His first time.

"It should be whatever we want it to be."

I don't know if I'm taking him at his word because it's the right thing to do or because I want it too much to deny him. Either way, I'll make sure he doesn't regret it.

When I get to his bedroom door, Miller is naked and reclining on pillows in the middle of his bed. One hand is stroking his cock and the other is caressing the inside of his thigh. Lube and condoms are scattered on the pillow beside him.

"Someone's in a hurry."

"Are you complaining?" Miller's smile is mischievous, as if he's just discovered his appeal and he wants to see how far he can push it.

All the way.

But he doesn't get to know that yet. Not until I get him on the same desperate page.

I walk over to stand by the side of the bed and drop the blue cord beside him.

When he sees it, he licks his lips as his eyes flicker from hazel to gold. "I know they weren't that hard to find. What took you so long?"

"You are not going to rush this." I tug my shirt off over my head. "You asked me to tie you to this bed, which means you trust me and know I'd never do anything to hurt you."

I shuck off my shoes and jeans while he watches with wide eyes. "But you need to know I'm not going to let you rush this. No matter how much you try to distract me. No matter how much you beg. Now get your hand off your cock and grab the bedpost."

I hold my breath, waiting to see how he takes the command. If I sense any hesitation or worry, I'll pull back. He asked for this and I want it, but what he needs is more important now.

Excitement glints in his eyes as he lifts his arms over his head. “I can’t believe I’m doing this.”

Thank you, God.

“Neither can I. You keep surprising me. I like it.”

And I love seeing his body spread out for me like a feast. He’s fit and hung, the olive skin slightly paler around his dark, straining erection. There are more freckles on his chest, along with fine blond hair I want to run my fingers through.

I’m no virgin. I haven’t been since high school. I’ve wanted sex, wanted release, and in the past, I wasn’t that choosy about the women who gave it to me.

But I crave Miller. Not just his body, though it’s doing things to me I can’t deny. But seeing him like this, knowing him as well as I do and thinking about all the things I’m going to do to him, is enough to bring me to the brink.

He has no idea how much he owns me.

I grab the cord with fingers that aren’t quite steady and wrap it around his wrists before knotting it to the iron bars of his old-fashioned headboard.

“You’re good at that.”

"Amsterdam," I say by way of explanation, unwilling to go into details. I'd rather show him.

Miller tugs a little, his lips parting as his breath speeds up at the snug restraint. "I didn't think this through. I want to touch you," he says almost plaintively.

"After," I promise, possessive tenderness welling up inside me. "As much and as long as you want."

He nods, his eyes already dilating with desire. He's giving me exactly what I want—total trust.

I cover his body with mine, lying on top of him with my hands gripping his and our lips a breath apart.

"I've got you now, Miller Day. Those talented hands won't distract me from all the wicked things I'm going to do to you."

He tugs again, almost as though he can't help himself. "What are you going to do to me now?"

"Anything I want." I rub my lips against his. "I have so many ideas. Tying you up is actually tame compared to some of the fantasies you've starred in."

There's disbelief in his beautiful eyes.

"It's true. I've got a vivid imagination when it comes to the firsts I want to give you."

"You can give me all of them," he offers, his voice

shaky but certain. "I want them with you."

"Fuck, Miller." With a few words, he's nearly destroyed my control again.

My kiss is punishing and openly carnal. I want him begging, I need him begging before I beat him to it.

I love the taste of him, his groans vibrating against my tongue and his erection digging into my stomach as he grinds against me.

I drag my lips along his neck, tracing his collarbone with my tongue before moving down to his small, hard nipples. He gasps and I suck gently, discovering how sensitive they are.

"I'll have more fun with these later," I promise, sliding further down the bed to sample his stomach, leaving a path of bite marks that make him squirm in arousal.

I love having my mouth on him. My hands on his skin. His reactions are honest and addictive, and the noises he makes have me lingering, learning him. I could spend days like this.

When I slide my hand up his inner thigh to cup him, he lifts his hips off the bed in silent demand. "Brendan, please."

"I thought you liked teasing," I say wickedly,

blowing softly against his cock. The arousal pearling at the tip of his shaft makes me lick my lips, hungry for a taste.

Next time.

"Why would you think a crazy thing like that?"

I almost grin at that. I told him I wouldn't let him rush me, but I'm having a hard time following my own rules. Every new taste and touch is making me more impatient. I want him too much.

I grip his thighs and lift, pressing his knees against his chest, and the view steals my breath. His ass cheeks are spread just enough to tempt me.

"This is going to be a first for both of us," I warn him, my breath rasping in my chest. "I'm glad you've got something to hold on to."

Miller struggles slightly in my grip when I lower my head. "What are you—? Brendan, *whaohmyfuckinggod!*"

My eyes close as I lick the tender skin between his cheeks, tasting the lube I didn't know was flavored and smiling against his skin at the noises he's making.

Cherry-flavored Miller.

I didn't lie—this may be my first time, but it's also one of my favorite fantasies. After my reaction to his ass in those boxers, I've been imagining that night going differently. Instead of saying things I don't mean, I drop to my knees and bury my face between those cheeks instead.

This is what I wanted. Miller at his most vulnerable. The tight ring of muscles I want to explore, the place I want my cock to call home. I memorize it with my tongue, biting and sucking on the tight flesh around the hole until he's swearing. Then I slide two fingers inside, stretching him so he can take more as I lick around them.

God, I could fuck him like this. With my tongue. Could I get deep enough to get him off with my mouth? Just feast on the tight bud until he comes again?

"Fuck me, Bren. Please fuck me," he begs hoarsely.

At his plea, I rock against the mattress, wanting that more than anything. But I hesitate, loving his reaction to my tongue.

"I need your cock inside me, damn it."

I lift up at that, snag a condom and rip the package with my teeth, taking in his red face and swollen lips. *So fucking sexy.*

I won't be able to last if I'm looking into those golden eyes while I bury myself inside him for the first time. "I need you on your knees."

There's enough give in the cord, though I know it

tightens when I reach for his hips and flip him over. "Too much?"

"It's good," he says breathlessly. "I love it. Don't stop now."

I don't think I can. I barely recognize myself as I roll on the condom and guide my stiff erection home. "I'll try to go slow."

He shakes his head rapidly, muttering under his breath as I slide one hand up his back to his shoulder and push forward.

Fuckfuckfuckfuck.

"Son of a bitch," Miller groans.

I stop, every cell in my body protesting. "You okay?"

"It's a lot." His laugh is choppy. "You're a lot. Just getting used to it."

"Can you take more?"

Don't say no.

Miller sends me a hot, frustrated look over his shoulder. "I'm tied up, aren't I? You're the one who decides what I can and can't take."

It's like waving a red cape in front of a bull. He doesn't understand how close I am to losing it. I dig my fingers into his shoulder and squeeze his hip with my free hand. "A wild streak *and* mouthy?"

"You bring it out in me," he says, lifting his hips higher in submission.

"Fuck." I press forward with one steady, forceful thrust that has me flush against his ass. "*Fuck,* that's perfect."

Miller is shaking, white-knuckling the bedpost, but he doesn't tell me to stop. He doesn't pull away. He's so damn tight, I feel like my head might explode. I want to shout loud enough for the whole damn city to hear.

"Mine. I got here first. Stay away."

I don't want to hurt him, but I need to move. I take some deep breaths and stare at the wall, trying to think of anything else to calm me down or this will all be over before it can start.

How can I think of anything else?

I drag my cock back and stroke deep. His moan of pleasure tells me to do it again. And again. And oh fuck, how did I not know it would be *this fucking good*?

"Now that I know how this feels, you won't be able to get rid of me." I watch my shaft disappearing in his ass and feel a growl building in my chest. "It's too good, Millie. Warm and tight." *And mine.* "You'll have to lock your bedroom door if you want me to stay away."

"Oh God, that's hot," he mutters, just loud enough

for me to hear.

"You like hearing that? Knowing I'll be thinking about this every time you walk by? Wondering when I can get back inside?"

"Yes," he breathes. "I love hearing it."

I love it too. Love that I'm the only one who knows how this feels. How tightly his muscles are squeezing me. How much he likes it when I lift my hand from his shoulder to tangle it in his messy hair.

I'm the only one who knows how hard he can take it.

He pushes back against me, begging until my hips are slamming against him in a punishing rhythm. *Harder. Deeper. Fuck, I can't get deep enough.*

"*Harder*."

"I have to—*need* to…" I can't focus on anything but how good he feels stretched around me. How much I need to come.

I hear the creak of the old bedpost as he grips it tighter, his cries and the sounds of slapping skin as I take more.

Faster. Harder.

"Yes. I'm almost— Damn it, Brendan. *Touch me*."

I have just enough awareness left to slip my arm under him and grab his thick cock, jerking roughly in time with my jarring rhythm. "Come for me first, Millie. Need you to come."

"Don't stop," he moans. "Brendan, I'm almost there."

"Get there, baby. Let me feel you come on my cock."

Miller's body arches in my grip and he cries out my name as he comes in my hand. My fingers are slippery with it. Covered in the proof of his release.

So good. God, it's so good it might really kill me. "Fuck."

My body curls around his, my thrusts brutal and bruising as I desperately reach for my climax. Can't hold back. I'll never get deep enough.

"*Yes*!"

I shudder, the force of the release crashing through me. Wave after wave of pleasure and relief as I pump inside his ass again and again. I can't stop stroking him. Can't stop fucking him. His body bucks against me with each pulse through my cock until it finally recedes, leaving me shaken.

I'm not sure how long I stay like that, deep inside and clutching him like a lifeline until I feel recovered enough to let go.

When I pull out gently, he shivers in reaction. I run my hand over his back and squeeze his hip before I get rid of the condom. Then I climb up the bed to untie the cord and rub circulation back into his arms.

I need to take care of him. I need to touch him and make sure I wasn't too rough.

God, was I too rough?

I knew it would be different. I knew we'd be good together. I had no idea need could be like that. So strong it was almost violent. Raw and revealing. I've never felt this naked after sex before.

Is it because it was Miller or because this was my first time with a man?

You already know the answer.

It isn't easy to admit it, even to myself. I can say I love him. I can say I want him. But *in* love? *That* kind of love? In the past, the mere idea of it would send me flying out of the country.

But I've already proven there's nowhere I can go that would be far enough to get Miller out of my head or my heart. He's there to stay, even though I know he's the kind of man who would need someone he was in love with to stick around.

Does Miller want me sticking around? Did I scare him again?

Ask him.

"You're quiet," I say tentatively.

Miller breathes out a laugh and buries his face in my shoulder. "I'm processing. Or maybe I'm dead. It felt like it for a minute there."

"Did I hurt you? Things got kind of intense. Was the cord too tight?"

"No. I mean, yeah, but in a good way. It was just what I needed. I had no idea sex would be that…*that.* Thank you."

That what? And *thank you*? What the hell does that mean? Who politely thanks you for banging their brains out?

"It's not this good with everyone," I say firmly, feeling like a needy asshole. "It's never this good."

He sighs sleepily. "Well, you would know."

I tighten my arms around him, needing a minute or two to compose myself before I blurt out something that— "I was jealous of Robbie. That's why I followed him."

Way to not blurt.

He stiffens, but I keep going. "That was when I knew I wanted you. That I had for a while. I haven't slept with anybody since then."

"Is this part of the afterglow experience people talk

about? I'm new to this, so I just want to be sure we're supposed to talk about other people we've almost slept with two minutes after seeing God."

He sounds wide awake now.

Good job, Brendan. At least he saw God before you ruined it this time.

He sits up, dragging the covers over his lap, his lips still swollen and distracting. I want to kiss him again. "Why did you tell me that, B? Are you the one freaking out over there? This *is* your first time with a man. Any regrets?"

"I should be asking you that—it's your first time with anyone," I remind him defensively. "But no, no regrets here. And I'm not freaking out now, but back then I was. I even went to a club in London to see if it was all men or just you I was attracted to."

When will you stop talking?

Miller runs a hand through his hair and shakes his head. "If you're about to tell me a story about experimenting at a gay club with another guy, I might kick you out again. I've had to deal with your X-rated Travelocity stories for years. At least those gnomes were women."

"No." I reach for his hand and slide my fingers

through his. "That's what I'm trying to say. The whole time I was there, I was thinking about you. It's just you, Millie. You're the only one I want."

He looks down at our hands, his brow crinkling again. "You don't have to say that. I wasn't holding out for a confession or a declaration of true love. I'm not experienced, but I'm not naïve either. We're friends. We had fantastic sex. I'm okay with that."

I'm not. Why the hell is he?

When I don't respond, he leans over and kisses my chest, my neck. When he straddles me, my cock responds because it can't resist him. I can't resist him. "What are you doing?"

"Let's try this again, Kinkaid."

Our kiss is long and slow, almost tender—more like a first time than our first time was. Without a word, he opens another condom, rolls it down my shaft and lowers himself on me with a soft moan.

I roll him over, looking into his eyes as we take each other back to the edge.

When I come, his mouth is on mine so I can't say the words that are trying desperately to escape my lips.

I love you.

But I fall asleep with them still lingering in my head.

A sound cracks through the room and Miller is off the bed and jumping into the nearest pair of sweatpants before I realize that what I heard. It sounded like a small explosion.

"What the hell?"

"Fred's house!" Miller shouts, racing out the bedroom door, his bare feet pounding down the stairs. "Call the fire department!"

I juggle my phone and my pants, flames from across the street tinting the room with hues of orange and gold while I give the address to the operator.

I glance out the window and see a shadowed figure running toward the burning house. I know it's Miller and I bolt after him down the stairs, desperate to catch up.

He's going to run into that damn house.

I cross the threshold of the front door and hear Diane and Heather scream Miller's name from the other side of the street. They're waving frantically, with Fred between them in a t-shirt and boxer shorts, Dix cuddled close to her chest.

Her eyes are wide and filling with tears.

Miller, thankfully sees them and runs over, pulling Fred into his arms.

"Is your sister inside?" I hear him ask as I run up to join the group, my bare feet slapping the asphalt. Miller glances at me, his expression grim but ready.

She shakes her head, crying too hard to speak. I step closer and send a questioning glance to Diane, whose face is twisted with rage.

"Fred's sister and her boyfriend were home tonight," she says through gritted teeth as she stares at the burning house. Flames have started to lick out the front door. We hear a loud whoosh, followed by glass shattering which makes us all flinch in surprise. Miller immediately starts urging them back across the street, further away from the fire.

Once we're standing on the grass in front of Miller's house I look back at Diane, "We heard them screaming at each other from across the street," she says bitterly, her eyes still fixed on the flames. "Fred was in her room, but she thinks they were cooking something on the stove because the fire started in the kitchen. While she was trying to put it out, they got in his car and left her behind." She hugs Fred protectively and gently pulls the sobbing girl's head to rest in the crook of her neck as Heather rubs her back. "Just left a fifteen-year-old girl alone inside a burning building."

Motherfucker.

Miller looks at me over the sobbing teenager, his expression furious.

I get out my phone, knowing exactly who I need to call.

Hopefully he's forgiven me by now.

CHAPTER EIGHT

Guinea Pigs and Barbecue

"How's Fred holding up?"

Royal and I are sitting at the bar on the far side of Finn's pub while Miller, Austen and a handful of her friends and family help set up for her first official Thursday night GPP.

Miller told me it was originally called a Guinea Pig Party—when it was just a family gathering where Austen could try out new products on her siblings and gossip—but she'd decided to change the meaning of the initials for its public debut. I think she's already scrapped Girl Power, Great Powder, and Getting Paid Party so far. She's supposed to be holding a family vote today.

If anybody's asking, I thought it was fine the way it was. But then, I don't spend much money on face creams.

"Fred's a champ," I tell Royal, twisting the cap on my water bottle. Yes, water. There's no way I'm drinking alcohol again for a while. Not here at the scene of the crime, anyway. "*We've* been more upset this week than she has. Even when they found her sister, she kept her cool. Thanks for calling in that favor by the way."

"Of course, man." He pats my shoulder sympathetically. "That's what brothers-in-law are for. Especially when they work for the real-life equivalent of Batman. I'm only sorry about how it turned out."

Yeah, about that. Fred's sister is a drugged-up waste of space, in my opinion. One who, even after seeing her boyfriend put in jail, has no desire to clean up her act, or maintain her status as Fred's legal guardian.

"The little she-boy can rot in hell. I'd rather go to jail than deal with her shit anymore. Took all my fun money to rent that place, and she flushed my stash like five times."

Which is when we found out exactly how Fred had gotten her sister to rent a house in the nice, decent neighborhood in the first place. The brilliant little model of civil disobedience had threatened to report her big sister, and her dirt bag boyfriend, for child endangerment and drug possession if she didn't spend Fred's half of their monthly trust stipend on a clean place to live until she could file for emancipation in six months.

Miller was right. She's very mature for her age.

"It'll work out." I gesture toward the laughing group across the room to change the subject. "It was nice of the owner to let Austen throw her first party here. I can't believe he closed the place down for this. At the last minute, no less."

Royal's face transforms with the slightly besotted grin I've come to expect whenever anyone mentions Austen's name. The man has it bad.

"Well, Austen's little brother, Thoreau, is Seamus Finn's business partner. He's a great guy, *and* he has a vested interest in keeping his young beer genius happy. She called Seamus as soon as she found out the hotel overbooked to see if they could work something out." Royal shrugs. "Besides, there could be some women in this group who decide to come for the pore cleanser but stay for the hot guys and beer. Pub makeovers could go viral."

I smile at the idea, feeling only moderately guilty for

being grateful to have a break from the cloud that's been hanging over the house since the fire.

Every night when we close the bedroom door, Miller is mine. He gives himself to me with no reservations. We can't get enough of each other. When I'm with him like that, it's raw and honest and I know there's nothing that could ever come between us.

Unfortunately, we don't stay in the bedroom twenty-four hours a day. And outside of that room, Miller is using his worry about Diane and Heather's anxiety, Fred's bravado, and his job at the day spa to keep me at a distance.

I'm not sure how to close the gap.

"Speak of the devil's husband," Royal booms jovially, and several people turn to see two men walking in the front door, hand in hand.

The older man has a handsome lumberjack thing going on, muscle-bound and bearded. The younger guy will now forever be the first image I think of when I hear the words *millennial hipster*. Cute though. He's definitely cute.

He has to be Royal's brother, JD Green. Which means the lumberjack old enough to be the cool uncle I always wanted is his husband, Carter Willis. Royal told me he used to be a drill instructor in the Marines.

I thought he'd look meaner.

As Royal introduces them, I realize that while they don't look like they go together at first glance, as soon as I see them interact—or notice the way Carter looks at JD like he's the only one in the room—it all makes perfect sense.

Just like it makes sense that Royal and J.D. are brothers as soon as they start bickering.

"Hello, lover boy." JD raises his voice. "How's your secret affair with Austen Wayne going? Been locked in any more rooms together?"

When Austen's sisters look over at us and laugh, I wince in sympathy, but Royal takes it in stride. "Hey, remember when you lived on the other side of the country and never called? Good times, right?"

JD turns to his husband. "Isn't *he* the one who's started looking for property in *our* neighborhood? That was him, right?" he says, hooking a thumb towards Royal.

Carter chuckles. "Okay, let's take it down a notch. We're here to be supportive." He glances at Royal and winks. "And to let JD find out more about your new girlfriend."

"I don't know what you're talking about. Mother Matilda didn't send me on a recon mission. I'm innocent. Just here to get a free massage and some skin toner." JD smiles warmly at me and holds out his hand. "Speaking of massages, nice to finally meet you in person, Desperado. I'm hoping you have stories about Royal's hijinks with broads abroad. I need more blackmail material."

I grin back, playing along. "Oh, I have stories."

"So do I, friend," Royal warns lightly.

Where's the trust, man? As if I would give his brother any more ammunition after that texting disaster.

"Carter, let's get JD a drink while we let Austen know you're here."

Carter gets a nod from JD before letting Royal drag him away.

"That wasn't obvious at all," JD says as he grabs the stool beside me. "I wish Fiona was here."

"Fiona?" I ask politely, since I have no idea who he's talking about.

"Best bartender-slash-psychologist I know." He grimaces. "She's having issues with her love triangle—a Finn *and* a Wayne, that greedy girl—so she's decided to take a break from both of them to audit a few classes this semester in sunny California. Meanwhile, I've been asked to help you without backup. If she were here, she could take the heat and tell you what you're doing wrong with your man."

I'm not sure I like where this is going. "What am I doing wrong? And who asked you for help?"

"My brother. The big, irritatingly cheerful one. He's worried about you."

"Why?"

"Oh, I don't know. You're suspended and technically homeless, you're having sex with your best friend, and now you're suddenly looking after a complicated teenager and a tiny energetic dog after a lifetime of carefree bachelorhood. Pick your poison."

I guess Royal's mentioned me once or twice.

JD sends me a sideways glance, his fingers tapping on the bar. "And you do need my help with Miller. It's early days yet, but he's already got that look. It's not a good sign."

"What look?" I turn toward Miller, who's deep in conversation with one of Austen's sisters. "He looks good. He looks fine."

As if sensing my attention, Miller turns to meet my gaze. His smile wobbles for a second before it turns into a full-fledged grin that makes me want to drag him out to that damn Hyundai for more semi-private time.

"Well that's good to know," JD says with a relieved sigh. "You love him, so half the battle is won. It might be a good idea to let him in on it."

I know he was right about the bungee cord, but come on. "What makes you so sure I haven't?"

JD pushes his hair behind his ears and shrugs. "If you'd told him you love him, he wouldn't be looking around every five minutes to make sure you haven't disappeared."

Is he doing that?

"He's having great sex for the first time ever—I'm just assuming it's great, since I'm not psychic, but I know you tied him up and I've heard stories about you for years. So if I were experiencing this late-blooming love fest with a hot guy I cared about? I would probably be floating around with a soft, fuzzy sexed-up glow. But there's no glow happening with Miller. He looks worried."

I scowl because I know it's true. Haven't I been wondering what's wrong? Why he keeps pushing me away?

"So you're saying it's because I haven't told him?"

"What do you think?"

Honestly? Whether or not it's fair to him, I think he should know me well enough to have an idea what I'm feeling. I'm here. I helped build the deck. I've picked up dog vomit. I've taken Fred to a protest and dealt with Diane's constant glowering.

But you haven't told him you want to stay. You haven't told him you love him.

There's been a lot going on. It's not like there's been a good time in the last week to…

Shit.

"I guess I really do suck at romance."

Royal sets a glass down on the bar in front of JD and squeezes my shoulder. "You really do. But you're getting better."

"Don't patronize him," JD says.

"It's called encouragement," Royal corrects. "Positive reinforcement. I learned that from my other brother Joey. He's a professional babysitter," he adds in a stage whisper to me.

JD rolls his eyes. "He owns the company."

"Whatever."

I get to my feet. "I need to go talk to Miller for a minute."

Carter smiles and slips his arm around JD affectionately. “Good man.”

“Wait.” JD’s eyes widen. “You can’t just walk up to him and blurt it out. Not now.”

“Why not?” Royal asks helpfully.

Yeah. Why not?

“Not everybody needs a grand gesture.” Carter gives JD a look. “But there is something to be said for romance.”

“It’s a good thing you brought barbecue to this party or we’d have words,” JD tells his husband grumpily. “And Brendan doesn’t need to take out an ad in the paper. But he knows Miller better than we do, and if he stops to think about it for a minute instead of barreling ahead without considering the consequences…”

He leaves his sentence unfinished, but I know where he’s going with it. Miller already thinks I’m impulsive. If I just throw it out there, he’s not going to take it seriously. He won’t understand, or even believe that I want to stay with him once my two weeks are up.

His belief that this is temporary has come up before, but I wasn’t paying enough attention to put it together.

“I’m going to make you a Dix Balzack calendar next Christmas. In memory of your short stint as a dog

owner."

And *"The next time you visit, I'll throw a party on this deck you finished. It's perfect."*

"He thinks I'm leaving."

"Aren't you?" Royal said quietly. "Austen's already pointed out that leaving is kind of what we do for a living. You know I've already been thinking about taking shorter trips. Flights that cross the country instead of the pond. But you love those long hauls. You always have. Miller knows that."

I do. Or at least I did. Before Miller, I'd never found anything I loved as much as flying. There is nothing wrong with the world when you're soaring that high above it. It was better than sex. More vital to me than anything else I could imagine.

Until recently.

Miller needs to know that he's vital to me. That he matters too much for me to let go of what we're making together.

I lean my elbow on the bar and force myself to relax, glancing at Royal. "I'm not sure how you survived nine brothers, man. I'm impressed."

Royal smirks at JD. "They aren't all like him. But there were a few years of crazy town that I wasn't sure we'd make it out of alive. Think Oliver Twist meets Lord of the Flies."

His brother shakes his head. "Think Annie with an all-male cast. Our parents are the Warbucks."

"I don't think about musicals that often," I offer, reaching up to rub my neck absently. "But I get the point."

"Brendan?"

Miller is waving me over, so I straighten. "Duty calls. Thanks for the advice, JD."

"Anytime, Desperado. Carter and I are going to bring in that barbecue now. Good luck."

I have a feeling Desperado might be my new nickname.

When I cross the room, Miller takes my hand without a word and leads me down a private hallway.

"Does she need to bring in any more boxes?" I ask curiously. "I thought we got everything."

He puts his hands on my shoulders and presses something that makes me sag against the wall. "Oh, shit, that's the spot. How did you know?"

"It's my job to know. And I needed an excuse to touch you. You didn't have to come to this."

"Yes, I did. Royal told me to." I pull him close and

slide my hands beneath his pants to grab his ass. "I love these sweatpants."

And you.

"Good, because I have about twenty pairs and I'm not giving them up."

When he kisses my neck, my dick stirs. "Is it bedtime yet?"

"It's your fault I agreed to this, so no. I'll only be a few hours. There can't be that many people getting a free massage. Then we can grab Dix and go home."

"We could grab dicks right now. No one's paying attention." I leer playfully, but not all of me is kidding.

"Speaking of…" He leans closer and lowers his voice. "Austen might have told me something about Royal. I'm not going to repeat it, because apparently that's not allowed, but you should know our one attempt at matchmaking? *Huge* success."

I laugh. "Good to know."

"No, I'm serious. *Huge*."

I yank him firmly against my erection. "That better be me you're talking about."

He bites his lip, mischief back in his eyes. "I'm not sure, but I think there's a private office around here somewhere if you want to refresh my memory."

We find a storage closet instead.

"I can't believe we're doing this," he mutters as we close the door behind us and I turn on the bare bulb that's dangling overhead. "The party is about to start any minute."

"You started it," I tell him, unbutton my jeans with an embarrassing amount of eagerness, since I just had him a few hours ago. The man drives me crazy.

"That's right." He leans against the door, watching my progress avidly. "You were reminding me how big you were."

"Huge was the word," I correct him, taking myself out with a hiss of relief.

His hand is inside his sweatpants, stroking himself at the sight of me until I stop him. "Didn't I tell you that was my job?"

"Then why aren't you doing it?"

I let go of my cock, tugging down his sweatpants and boxers until they're clinging to his thighs. The head of his cock is already wet with arousal and it makes my mouth water. "Quick and dirty. No one will notice we're gone."

I wouldn't care if they did. The surprised, pleased look Miller always gets in his eyes when he tempts me like this is worth any embarrassment.

He still doesn't know he's irresistible. Something else I need to convince him of.

I lick my palm and wrap my fist around our cocks, tightening my grip until he moans into my hand. "Touch me, Miller. You can give your magic hands and attention to everyone else in a minute. But right now I need to remind you that you belong to me."

When his hands coast over my back beneath my shirt, I exhale roughly. "I love your hands, Millie. I love how hard you get for me."

I love you.

I run my thumb over the head of his cock and revel in the feel of his shudder, reaching up to cover his mouth with my free hand when his moan echoes in the small room. "Quiet now or someone might hear us."

He moans louder into my hand as I jack us off.

"Is your wild streak showing again? I can let go if you want me to. If we had time, I'd turn you around and lick that sweet ass until you were screaming for God again. Is that what you want?"

He shakes his head, but his eyes are all black with gold edges. Part of him loves the idea.

"I don't want to share you," I whisper in his ear, my

hand still over his mouth as I stroke him faster. "Those screams are for me. I'm the first and last one to make you come. Always."

Miller whimpers and I feel my climax closing in.

"Don't let them hear you," I warn, releasing my grip and dropping to my knees to take him in my mouth.

"Fuck," Miller cries. Then he slaps his own hand over his mouth as I swallow him down my throat.

Love you. Love you. I'm keeping my mouth busy so I won't shout it. Won't spill my guts in a storage closet at a bar.

Don't you know, Millie? I'm not going anywhere.

He grips my head as he comes, his shouts muted by his fist.

One more stroke of my cock is all it takes for me to join him, then I press my head against his hips as I recover.

"Wild streak," I say, kissing his thigh before I get to my feet. "A delicious, salty wild streak."

I lick my lips and he flushes, tugging up his pants as he looks around the small closet. "You're a bad influence."

"I don't know. I'm not the one who keeps suggesting public places to get off in."

He whacks my back as I open the door to check out the hallway.

"All clear," I say, smiling. As I step out, my phone starts to buzz in my pocket. "Huh."

"I bet it's Royal trying to triangulate our location. Or his brother, the advice columnist."

It would have to be. Other than the people in this pub, no one else calls me unless it's about work or there's some kind of emergency. "Hold that thought."

I pull out my phone and swipe the screen, then stare blankly at the caller ID. "This has been the weirdest week," I mutter.

Miller reaches for my hand and tilts the phone so he can see the screen. "Oh."

Right?

For the first time in five years, my father is calling.

In hindsight, I should have let it go to voicemail.

Chapter Nine

Not That Kind Of Happy Ending

Miller

"Are you sure you're ready for such a big commitment?" Phoebe asks, looking worried. "People shouldn't make decisions like this in the heat of the moment. Britney Spears is the perfect example."

For the first time in days, I'm fighting a smile. I think I finally managed to shock the stylists. Three of them are staring at me as if I walked in off the street and requested a penis piercing. Phoebe, the little blonde I asked for a haircut, just looks at me like she's not sure whether I'm in my right mind.

Not that boring anymore, am I?

"This isn't a heat-of-the-moment decision. I've been working here for three years now. It's about time I *indulged* myself, don't you think?"

Nothing but crickets.

"Get it? Indulgence?"

I thought it was funny, but they're all still looking at me like stylish guppies with their mouths hanging open.

"I'm free now. I'll do it." Betty, the redhead I've always had pegged as the ringleader, finally closes her mouth and walks up to me, gently nudging her blonde friend out of the way.

She lifts her arms to run her fingers through my hair with a familiarity I wasn't expecting. "I've been wanting to get my hands on this for a while now. You don't dye it at all? No highlights? This is natural?"

I'd nod if she didn't have such a vice-like grip on my head. "People have always assumed I couldn't make up my mind when it came to hair dye, but I swear it's all mine."

She laughs. It's genuine too, which is surreal. Damn it, do I have to stop calling them Mean Girls?

"Come into my parlor." *Said the spider to the fly.*

She pats the back of her barber chair. "I'll give that hobo nest a style worthy of those gorgeous colors."

Thank God, the world is still round and she's still a little catty, or this would definitely feel like a trap.

I sit down and she swoops a cape over me, snapping it around my neck. It's tight. I thought these were one size fits all. "I have an hour until my next appointment."

"In an hour, you won't be able to recognize yourself."

I think she missed the boat on that because it's already happened.

Has it only been a week and a half since Brendan showed up drunk at the pub? So many things have changed since then.

I hear the slightly ominous sounds of snipping near my ear and the hum of conversation as the other stylists go back to their appointments. Then my personal inquisition begins. "It's a guy, isn't it? Why you're finally getting this done? I hope it's not to impress him. I always say if a man doesn't like me exactly as I am, he can go suck a lemon."

Once again, not shaking my head. She has scissors. "You've also always said I needed a haircut."

And new clothes. And a life that included a man.

Betty snorts as she works on her masterpiece. "True. We *have* given you a hard time, Miller. But only because we were worried about you. You've never looked as good as you will when I'm through with you, but a few months after you started working here, you kind of…" The snipping stops as she hesitates.

"Let myself go?" I offer helpfully. That was just after my mom died.

"Yeah." She sighs and starts cutting again. "I think a prerequisite of this job is being nosy. There's nothing worse than a quiet stylist, right?"

I can think of one or two things. "Right."

"And whether you know it or not, mister, you are very popular up here. All our regulars rave about your massage skills. I've been tempted to make an appointment myself, but I'm so busy with this job, my two kids and the in-laws who decided to move in right across the street—thank you very much—I have a feeling that if I ever let myself relax I'd fall asleep and not wake up until retirement."

This is the most she's talked to me in three years. I didn't even know she was married. "I know what you mean."

And I do. Whether she knows it or not, I've got a lot going on in my life right now. My virgin years ended with a vengeance. I have a new deck. A new dog. A Fred.

She wants me to be her legal guardian. *Me.*

That's one of the reasons behind my sudden desire to get an actual haircut instead of trimming it myself. And yes, that's what I've been doing.

Relax, it's just hair.

I've always been responsible. I have a decent nest egg growing for my retirement, a house in my name, a car I don't owe anything on and a skill set that insures I'll always have a job. But I need to *look* more respectable.

I know how big a deal this is. And I made sure Fred knows that if I sign on to this, I'm not going to be a hostel she squats in until Emancipation Day. I'll want her to stay, graduate from high school and get into a good college. I want her to be able to do something with all that brainpower. Maybe even change the world.

I have no doubt she can do it.

Taking Fred on isn't entirely selfless. Having her around on a permanent basis would be good for me. It would help get me out of my own head and out of this funk I've fallen into since Brendan left.

Three days. He went to see his father three days ago, and he hasn't gotten back yet. Most of his luggage is still here, but with only two days left of his two-week suspension, it's getting pretty clear that I need to get used to life without him again. To be good with short, sporadic visits and the way things used to be.

I can do that.

So far I'm not handling it as well as I'd like. But the brand-new case of insomnia I suddenly developed has given me enough time to do a quick renovation of the guest bathroom in case Fred decides to stay. So, that's kept my mind off my heartbreak and the empty bed I couldn't sleep a wink in last night. I wonder what I'll have to do this time.

Betty is still chatting, and I tune back in just in time to catch the tail end of her monologue. "I heard her product party was a success, but I had no idea she'd made enough to suddenly go flying off to Paris."

"What? Who are you talking about?"

"Austen Wayne," Betty says. "I've been talking about her for five minutes."

"Who told you Austen is flying to Paris?"

She would have told me if she were making plans like that, right? I just talked to her last night and she didn't say anything other than she wouldn't be in today.

Betty waves her arms expressively and I worrying about random eyes getting poked out. Maybe my legal guardian instincts are already kicking in.

"Nina at the front desk?" she says, lowering her voice to a conspiratorial tone. "Austen called and Nina heard her tell the boss she was still paying for her space, but she'd be gone for a week. Paris was mentioned. I thought you two were friends. Didn't she tell you?"

I dip into my pocket for my phone and try to send a quick text without Betty reading it.

Me: *Paris?!*

Austen: *I thought you didn't listen to gossip.*

Me: *Getting my haircut upstairs. See? We both keep secrets.*

Austen: **&%$!!!*

Me: *So…Paris?*

Austen: *Long weekend, Cupid. He handed me tickets this morning. Am I insane?*

Royal. That son of a bitch is good. But he's also a good match for her. I've never seen two people come together this easily before. Like they've been dating for years instead of days.

Like they fit.

"Confirmed," I say out loud. "Austen is going to Paris with Royal."

Shit. I think the fumes in the salon have actually gotten to me.

That's my story. Go with it.

"*Who* is Royal?" Betty asks immediately, reminding me of a shark circling chum.

Unfortunately, a woman in the middle of getting a dye job two chairs down speaks up. "If that's the sexy beast who was at her beck and call at the GPP last Thursday, then she's the luckiest girl on the planet. He was *huge*."

I snort and send Austen another message.

Me: *You can never come back here. They know.*

Austen: *I don't care. But you didn't answer my question.*

What am I supposed to tell her? Is flying to Paris with a man she's technically known only a few days insane? On paper, sure. But is it any more insane than falling for your straight best friend, then throwing yourself at him as soon as he gets curious and damn the consequences?

At least Austen's crazy has a happy ending.

Me: *Insane in the best possible way. Go. Drink wine, eat smelly cheese and stare at his glorious calves in Paris.*

Austen: *You think my calves are glorious too? I though you only loved me for my nail gun skills.*

Austen: *Sorry! He stole my phone. I'm going! Another Wayne bites the dust. What about you? Any news?*

Me: *I'll still be here when you get back. But with shorter hair.*

I put my phone away and try not to let feeling sorry for myself get in the way of my happiness for Royal and Austen.

Betty squeezes my shoulder. "You're a good friend."

Yep. She was definitely reading over my shoulder.

"I am," I say with forced lightness. "Remind me to tell you how I got those two together. And then got locked in a room for an hour."

She laughs and spins the chair around to face the mirror, unsnapping my cape with a flourish. "All done."

Before I look, I make myself a promise. This is a fresh start. A new haircut and a new Miller Day. It's time to grow up and face the truth about where things aren't going with Brendan.

My handsome pilot isn't taking me to Paris. Not that I want to go to Paris, but if I did, I'm pretty sure it would be on my own.

I was right about our lives being too different. The last few days have been a good example. I'm complaining about shelling out the money for a decent haircut and Brendan is likely at a country club having cocktails with his rich father's investors.

To be fair, I know he doesn't care about any of that, and for his sake I hope they can find some common ground. But either way, when it's done he'll go back to his carefree globetrotting life and, like I told Austen, I'll still be here.

Didn't you just say it was time for a new Miller Day? A fresh start?

The voice in my head is right. Maybe I'll start saving up for a vacation instead of another house project. The house is done. Why mess with perfection?

Who are you?

I have no idea.

"Are you ever going to look in the mirror, Miller?" Thankfully Betty sounds amused instead of irritated. "I can't gloat until you do. And I love to gloat."

I look in the beveled glass and have the strangest desire to pinch myself. "Holy shit."

Betty can be mean as a snake, but it's clear she knows what she's doing career-wise. I look like a new man. The haircut is short in the back and on the sides, the sweep in the front enhancing my natural red and gold highlights. I look more mature, despite the freckles. I don't want to say sexy but… "This is amazing."

"I know." Betty is practically dancing in her heels when a smattering of applause comes from the other stylists and their clients. "He looks like a cover of GQ now, doesn't he? I wish I'd taken a before and after picture. He was hiding so much hotness underneath that shag."

I'm not hiding anymore.

"Betty." Nina's voice comes over the PA system. "I can hear you up there. Please tell GQ his appointment is in room one."

I pull out my credit card but Betty waves it away. "You've already made my week, Miller. Just let me see your phone and we'll call it even."

I hesitantly hand her my phone, blushing when she takes a picture of me. Then she types something rapidly and hands it back with her trademark smirk.

She sent another message to Austen with my picture attached.

Me: *Betty is the best.*

_

Brendan

What is taking him so long?

I bribed the lady at the front desk to slip me into the private room before letting him know "his client" had arrived. She informed me that Miller was upstairs getting a haircut, so I was safe.

Why is he cutting his hair?

I've been racing around the room since then, stripping off my clothes, finding the switch to dim the lights and slipping a CD into the player—Peruvian flute, which is the sexiest music available at the moment. I'm working with a limited arsenal here.

Everything needs to be perfect.

I'm a man on a mission. The last few days with my father were like a high budget Scrooge reenactment in my honor.

Here's a ghost from your past, in the present, telling

you about your shitty future if you ever let yourself turn out like him.

The last time I'd talked to him—less than a year after my mother died—he asked me to sell back her stocks in the company. But after what he said yesterday, I made sure he paid what they were worth before I cut him out of my life for good.

I chose my real family a long time ago, and the conversations Miller's been having with me on the phone for the last few days—about starting a family of his own—showing me that now might be the perfect time to make it clear that I want to be a part of that future. With him.

Even JD would think this is romantic.

I hear steps in the hall and get in position on the massage table, covering my ass with a sheet and my head with the closest available pillow.

I hope he likes the surprise.

"Nina, did you turn on the—oh." There's a long pause, then I hear him pick up the clipboard with the fake name and details I scribbled on there while I waited.

"Mr. N. *Cage*?"

"Mm-hmm." I'm trying not to laugh, because yeah, Nicholas Cage.

"Mr. Cage," he says matter-of-factly, setting down the clipboard. "I'll admit I don't have many male clients, but I do know all about the lower back injury you say you're suffering from. Would you like to discuss what I intend to do, or should I just show you instead?"

Does that sound as suggestive as I think it does? He knows it's me, right? I mean, I don't have any tattoos or birthmarks, but if anyone can pick my body out of a lineup, it should be Miller.

Without revealing myself, I hold up two fingers.

"Option two. Great choice. I can't wait to get a feel for your problem."

Okay, he's got to be fucking with me.

When he doesn't rip the pillow away or give me hell for not letting him know I was coming back today, I'm honestly not sure what to do next.

Why do I try to plan things? They never go the way I expect them to.

When he starts rubbing the warmed oil into my tense arms, my shoulders, my back… What was I saying again?

The pillow muffles my groan of ecstasy. I can't even describe what he's doing, but he's finding and fixing aches I didn't know I had. I've never been this relaxed in my life. I'm even starting to dig the flutes.

Which is why it takes me a minute to react after his hands slip beneath the sheet and start to rub my ass.

"You're holding a lot of tension here, Mr. Cage," he purrs, kneading the cheeks in a way that makes my cock instantly swell and demand to be let in on the conversation.

What the fuck?

"Relax. You know, you remind me of someone, Mr. Cage. He was a hard ass too. Excuse me, *has* a hard ass. If he hadn't disappeared on me a few days ago, I might have done something like this for him."

He slides one warm, slicked-up finger through my crack, lightly glancing the sensitive nerves in between, and my entire body starts to heat up. I'm actually tingling.

"Jesus," I mutter.

"I think this is the kind of deep, thorough massaging he needed." His fingers return again and again. A small rub. A teasing circle.

Then he starts massaging the tight bundle of muscles and I'm so hard I can barely get the words out. "Do it."

"Mr. Cage?"

I toss the pillow on the floor and push up on one

elbow, twisting to reach for him. "Stop fucking teasing me and do it, Miller. Let me feel it."

I snag the back of his neck but there's nothing to grab onto. "Damn haircut," I grumble, pulling him down to kiss him in a way that leaves no doubt who I am and how much I've missed him.

"Do it," I repeat the command against his lips. "I know you've thought about it. Let's see if we can keep that wild streak going."

"Breathe out," he whispers, excitement deepening his voice as he pushes inside with his thick, slippery finger.

"Oh fuck," I gasp, my ass clenching at the invasion. "*Miller*."

"Relax." He kisses me again, almost breathing for me until I get used to the sensation.

"Don't stop." My voice is shaking. *I'm* shaking. I'm not even sure if I like it, but I need him to keep going. "Please."

His thrusts are slow and shallow at first, his other hand caressing my jaw, soothing me as he fingers my ass. "Let me know when you want more."

"More," I say immediately, not knowing if it's true. My dick thinks it is. I have to get up on my knees or risk leaving a permanent dent in the massage table.

"You like it." Miller's voice is almost hypnotic as he adds another finger to the first. "Don't you, Mr. Cage?"

I puff out a laugh and reach for his cock. "You've got too many clothes on, Mr. Smartass."

He pushes his sweatpants down and presses his thighs against the table near my face as he fucks me with his fingers. "Is that better?"

"Fuck, yes," I groan, straining to take him in my mouth. I wrap my arm around his hips and pull his body into my face, letting him fuck my mouth as he fucks my ass.

If I die with his fingers in my ass, his dick in my mouth and Peruvian flutes playing in the background, I'll haunt him, I swear to God. I'll die happy, but there will be haunting.

We're a jumble of moans and oil and body parts, sucking and touching and begging for more. Somehow, even during his climax, he's able to keep fucking my ass with his skilled fingers. Luckily, I lift my mouth from his cock before he starts massaging my prostate, because I come so hard I bite my tongue and nearly sprain my neck again.

"Fuck, Miller, that was…" I can't finish. He knows.

I'm not sure I have any muscles left in my body.

After the massage and that orgasm, it might be a while before I can get off this table.

"Welcome back," Miller says with a breathless laugh, adjusting his pants and reaching for a wet towel to wipe off his hands.

"Surprise," I say weakly from the massage table, or as I like to call it, my new home. "Honey, I'm home."

He doesn't respond to that, and I lift my head and set my chin on my crossed arms as he busies himself around the room. "I'm sorry it took three days to get back."

"I understand."

There's no way he can. "My father kept *accidentally* running into people he wanted me to meet. Do you know why he wanted to see me in the first place?"

"No. Why?"

"Good old dad seems to think I'm a viable commodity again, and he wants me to take a more active role in the company. Public relations, to be specific. And this is the good part," I say with a grimace. "It was all because of that damn video."

"You're an internet sensation, Brendan. Have you been in a cave? There's a petition for you to get a medal or a key to the city, if you can believe it. They're calling you Captain America. Why shouldn't we use that kind of

free publicity and goodwill to our advantage?"

Asshole.

"Did you say yes?"

"Did I—Are you listening to me, Miller?" A thought occurs to me and I stare at him in disbelief. "You thought I wasn't coming back, didn't you?"

Miller doesn't look at me, but seeing his profile now, I really do like that haircut. It makes me smile until he opens his mouth.

"I wasn't sure if you'd be able to get your things before you went back to work, flying off to parts unknown, no. But the surprise was nice."

"Okay, I'm greased up and naked, but we're doing this now."

He spins on his heel, looking nervous. "Doing what now? There's nothing we need to be doing."

"You know." I point at him and climb off the table, wrapping the sheet around my waist like a giant towel. "You know me and you know what it is that we've been doing together."

"Sex?"

I jam my hand through my hair. "Why are you making it less than it is? Why do you keep trying to push me out the door? Have I given you any mixed signals?

Acted like I was unhappy with how this was working out?"

He shakes his head, eyes just a little too wide. "There were no signals to mix. We're friends. We had se—"

"I'm in love with you, friend. How's that for a signal?"

Miller's expression closes and he moves quickly to the door. "No, you're not. Get dressed and we'll talk about this later."

"*No, I'm not*?"

I don't beat him to the door, but I'll be damned if that stops me from following after him. "Stop running away from me, Miller Day."

The murmurs that make the day spa machine run come to a screeching halt at the sound of my voice and Miller's face turns a shade of red I haven't seen before. "Get dressed," he grits out. "We're not talking about this here."

"We're not talking about it at home either. So why shouldn't we do it here? I've been told I suck at romance more times in the last few weeks than I want to admit, but here I am, making a grand gesture. Telling you I lo—"

"Don't."

One quiet word and it twists in my heart like a knife. I shake my head, suddenly tired. "You know what? You're worse at this than I am. You're more afraid of this than I am. At least I can say it. I love you. What's worse is that *you know it* because no one else knows me better than you do. I want to live in that house with you and Fred and Dix. I want *Diane* to be my neighbor, that's how far gone I am. I want to stay."

I take a breath, my chest heaving with the effort not to shake him when he still doesn't respond. "You're the one holding us back, Miller. I know how hard it was for you to lose your mother. It was hard for me too. But there's something special between us. There always has been. And you could have it if you'd stop pushing it away, but you have to make that decision. You're the one who has to tell me where we go from here."

The murmuring returns with a roar as I turn to grab my clothes. No doubt I just made everything worse by humiliating him at work, but I can't worry about that now.

All I can do is hope he heard me.

And maybe go get drunk again. That's always good for a laugh.

CHAPTER TEN

Roberta Don't Give Me No Flack

Miller

New deck. New haircut. New box-o-wine I got from the corner store on the way home. Oh, and the speakers I installed a few days ago that are sharing my love for a certain classic R&B singer with the entire neighborhood as we speak.

Jesse come home,
there's a hole in the bed, where we slept.
Now it's growing cold.

I'm not a pub guy. I'm a box-of-wine-by-myself guy. It's getting so pathetic my ridiculous dog decided to join Fred at Heather and Diane's house until I get my act together.

"It's only been a few hours," I mumble into my red plastic cup, because there's no way I'd risk drinking around sharp objects. I'm a lightweight, remember? "You'd think they'd be more understanding."

They actually were, until I gave them more details about what happened at work today. Once they realized what Brendan had done, everything that he'd said in front of the entire staff of Indulgence—who've been dying for any bit of interesting gossip about my life for years—he became the hero of the story. Me? I was the big, 'fraidy chicken. Cat. Whatever.

Even Diane.

She's never liked Brendan. She'd thought the same thing Regrettable Robbie had—that he was using what I felt for him, along with the memory of my mother, against me. Tugging on my heartstrings. Coming around whenever he wanted some affection and a home-cooked meal.

He'd be happy to know that she's done a one-eighty, and I'm the one on the receiving end of her stink eye now. And why? Because I didn't want to have an incredibly personal conversation at work?

Was it not as professional as getting a blowjob five

minutes earlier?

"The door was closed," I reason, filling another glass before lying on my back to look at the stars.

I keep going over what Brendan said. He has a point. I've been pushing people away. I've kept all of my focus on this old place, because I know if something goes wrong with it, I can fix it. A house can't get sick and waste away. A house can't fly off into the sunset and leave you.

So yeah, I've had some issues. But even if I didn't, how in the hell would *I* know how *he* felt? I'm not Austen. I'm not a witchy Sherlock woman. I can't read minds.

I'm also the one with zero experience at this. I knew *I* was in love with him, but was I supposed to intuit that he loved me back by his finger technique or the amount of times we came together in a single night?

Why are you making it less than it is?

"Because I didn't know it could be more." Anything I thought I saw, or might have felt coming from him, I put in the wishful thinking column of my heart. He'd been in that column for years. It was habit.

And I'm leaving the light on the stairs.
No, I'm not scared,

I wait for you.
Hey Jesse, it's lonely, come home

"Are you planning to torture us with this easy listening for the morbidly depressed all night?" Diane asks sharply from their upstairs window. "Don't you think Fred's been through enough trauma?"

"There's nothing easy about Roberta," I shout back, already knowing I'm going to be really embarrassed about saying that tomorrow.

"Could you two keep it down? It's a weeknight," says the neighbor who lives behind me. The one I've only spoken to once at a community meeting when he moved in a year ago.

"Sorry, Mr. James. But if you want me to turn off the music, I'm afraid I'm not going to be able to do that," I tell him, as politely as possible. "If you want to call the police, I can't stop you. I probably deserve it."

Because I suck at drinking. And relationships. Didn't Brendan say that to me the last time we fought? That I was wound too tight to be in a relationship? Well, he was right about that too.

"What's wrong with him?" Mr. James asks Diane casually, as if they aren't both shouting out their open windows.

These houses are too close together.

"A man he's in love with told him he loves him back. It's a tragedy, apparently."

"Can't you two use a phone?" I grumble, trying to focus on the lyrics that I'm starting to realize would make anyone suicidal.

Why am I listening to this? More importantly, why did *Mom* listen to this?

And she listened to it all the time. I can't even remember all the times I'd wake up in the middle of the night to *Killing Me Softly*, *Jesse* or *Where is the Love?*

God, even those titles are killing me. And not that softly.

Whenever people who knew Aurelia Day described her, the first word they used would almost always be joy. She was a *joy* to be around. No matter how sick she got, no matter how broke we were. Everyone loved her.

But at night she listened to these songs about broken hearts and missed opportunities.

Halfway into my box of liquid enlightenment, the only conclusion I can come to—and one that hits me like a wine-flavored freight train—is that she lied. Either by omission or with intent, my mother led me to believe she didn't regret anything, didn't miss anyone and she'd never really been in love.

But who listens to songs like this unless they're drowning some kind of sorrow? Unless they understand what it's like to be left behind?

Why didn't she tell me? We talked about everything.

Maybe because she didn't want to scare you with her drunken bouts of backyard melancholy. You know. Like you're doing every time Fred looks out that window.

"I'm sorry, Fred," I say too softly for her to hear over the fence. I haven't even filled out the official paperwork, and I've already failed as her legal guardian.

"It's okay."

I look up in surprise to find her standing just inside the sliding glass door, Dix sitting quietly at her feet. "Did you forget something? I thought I put the dog treats in his backpack."

But I've been focused on the whole drinking thing.

She joins me on the deck, taking off her ball cap and running a hand over her recently buzzed head. "I wanted to hang out with you, I guess. And I'm okay with the music. This singer reminds me of my mom."

"Me too. Mine, I mean."

Fred nods wisely. "I figured. I like that—I mean it blows, that we both lost our moms. But I like that you still have her pictures up, still listen to the music she liked. You know?"

I think Fred lost most of her family albums in that fire. What she has on her social media stream is it. We should print those out.

"I like to keep her memory alive," I say. "Pull it out whenever I need her. Although right before you came out, I was working my way up to being mad at her for not giving me better relationship advice. And this music is depressing."

She laughs and sits down next to me. "Brendan talks about her too. Your mom," she says quickly after mentioning his name. "He said the three of you were close."

"We were." Not *that* close or she wouldn't have told me on more than one occasion that sex and romance were overrated. She would have told me there was a chance that I could have both with someone who knew everything about me and wanted me anyway.

And if you were really close to Brendan, you would have known he was in love with you. At least, according to him.

"It's not because of me, is it?" she asks, tugging at the laces of her boots in a nervous gesture I've never seen her make before. "You didn't break up with him because I want to live with you? I hear I'm a lot to take on."

She says it lightly, but I can hear her doubts. She's so smart that sometimes I forget how young she still is.

I sit up, set my drink down and put my arm around her shoulder. "He said he wanted to live with *us*, Fred. Not just me. Us."

It surprised me, how quickly he adapted to having her around. He even wore the *Resist* shirt she'd gotten him. In public.

"It's not about you, I promise. You're wonderful. I'm the one that broke this."

My inner control freak was celebrating how right he'd been. How inevitable this was. Seriously, fuck that guy.

And yes, my mother was amazing. Best mom in the world. But I'm looking at my future now and there are some similarities I'm not that comfortable with. Will I be watching Fred grow up and possibly become the second or third female president of the United States—she would be mad if she were the first—with no one to share it with? Will I be listening to Roberta Flack while she sleeps, and wishing I hadn't let Brendan leave because I was too afraid to trust him when he said he wanted to stay?

Let's recap again. For Team Logic.

Brendan, the heterosexual playboy/pirate/pilot shows up with a dog. For me. Admits to wanting me without any hang-ups or hesitation. Deals with my neighbors. Builds my deck. Comes out to his friend. Handles first times and fires like a champ. Goes to a party where the women spend three hours discussing chin sag and large pores without a complaint. Surprises me at work to tell me he loves me.

I grab the remote and turn off the music.

"Oh good," Mr. James says with a relieved sigh.

I honestly forgot he was still there.

"I thought I might have to put some pants on," he continues. "To help straighten things out."

I can hear Heather laughing through the window while Diane tries to shush her.

"Where's my phone?" I ask Fred, patting my pockets. "I can't find my phone."

I stumble over the wine box when I get to my feet. Is the backyard spinning?

"About that," Fred says, her voice oddly muffled. "Your battery died? So Austen sent me an emergency text message."

"How does Austen have your number?"

Fred shrugged. "She signed one of my petitions a while ago. She's really involved in local politics, plus she makes my favorite body scrub."

She turns her screen toward me—not letting me hold it because I'm intoxicated and she's smarter than I am—and I squint hard, trying to make out the words.

Austen: *Tell M that B is at the airport ASAP! #SaveWatson*

"I'm not sure who Watson is," Fred says with a shrug. "But the rest of it sounded important."

He's at the airport? He's leaving tonight? He just got back today.

"I have to go there. I have to stop him."

"Fred, grab his keys and tackle him if you need to. We're coming over."

Diane's warning has me racing toward the sliding glass door. "No one is taking my keys alive!" I shout dramatically. "I have to tell him!"

I'm not sure what happened in the seconds that followed, but I saw a flash of fur and ended up on my back on the kitchen floor, right where I plan to eventually put a nice banquette.

"Airport," I wheeze.

"Well, that isn't happening," Heather says easily, hovering over me like an apparition. "Even if you could get in your car and drive without putting everyone else in danger, would you really want him to see you like this? You're in worse shape than he was. I think the both of you should just stop drinking entirely if this is the end result."

I rub my head. "*Ouch.* Did someone hit me?"

"Your little dog darted out in front of you, and you fell trying to avoid him," Diane says with a certain amount of satisfaction. "Nothing's broken, and it gave me time to hide your keys. You're welcome."

Dix is panting worriedly in my ear. Do dogs worry? Well, this one does. "It's okay, Ridiculous. I'll still love you. Even if he flies away before I can tell him what I need to and he starts dating a runway model. Even if I die alone."

"Oh, good lord," Diane mutters. "I had no idea wine made him so dramatic."

"What do you want to tell him?" Fred asks from somewhere behind me.

"It's a little personal," I say, closing my eyes and wondering if I have enough energy to bob and weave around my jailers, find my keys and get to the door without falling on my face.

Sounds doable.

"We won't tell." Heather picks up Dix and walks over to the sink. "I'll make some coffee while you practice."

Practice. I don't have to practice. I've had it in my head for years. "I'd tell him he answered my prayers in that hospital room and I've been grateful ever since. I'd thank him for saving me after Mom left. For being my friend, despite the fact that I push people away, I can't drink, can't be impulsive, and can't fly away with him when he leaves."

"Diane, are you *crying*?" Heather asks in a shocked, hushed voice.

"*No*. You know I don't do that."

I ignore them, imagining he's standing there, looking down at me and laughing at my current situation. "I'd thank him for forcing me to have fun. Making me laugh and showing me my wild streak. And I'd tell him I've loved him since the first time I saw him. I'd even sing it for him if he asked this time," I say with a smile, remembering. I might sing a few lines, I'm not sure.

"I really don't want him to leave."

Diane and Heather help me up off the floor and walk me over to the couch. I feel someone take my shoes off, and then a warm blanket being tucked in around me.

I want to thank them, but I'm already half asleep, dreaming of Roberta playing piano softly in the background, and Brendan's body curled around mine.

The first time, ever I saw your face...

_

Brendan

"Is he...singing...while lying on his kitchen floor?" Austen is quiet, trying not to draw too much attention at the crowded departure gate as she watches a video of Miller Day, drunk literally off his ass and singing a love song.

To me.

"He has a decent voice," Royal offers, for once not cracking a joke. "But why does he think you're going anywhere? We're the ones hopping on the plane."

That was the question. Well, it's was one of them. Another is, who's the unlucky SOB who gets to tell

Miller that Fred recorded his drunken confession and sent it to Austen via text?

Fred: *M would have told B this in person, if we'd let him have his keys. #WhoisWatson*

I stare in judgmental silence at Austen, and Royal joins me until she crosses her arms defensively. "What? How was I supposed to know he'd be too drunk to drive here? You were really upset when you showed up, Brendan, and I worried that he might be too. I wanted to help. Pay it forward, Cupid style."

Royal chuckles, sliding his arm going around her shoulder. "I think we should all quit the Cupid business. We'll never be able to top our first time."

She leans into him with a nod. "I hated the thought of him being miserable while I was in Paris, that's all."

"Don't worry," I say, looking down as the video starts to replay. "Can you send this to my phone?"

"Not if you're planning to torture him with it."

Royal kisses her forehead and slides the phone out of my hand, forwarding the video. "Don't worry, I didn't also send it to myself to pull out on their tenth wedding anniversary. I swear."

Our tenth? "He's drunk," I tell them weakly. "People say crazy things when they're drunk."

What if he changes his mind again in the morning? What if he still doesn't trust me enough to believe we stand a chance?

Don't act as if this is a choice. You already made yours.

Royal grips both my shoulders and shakes me.

Always the affectionate bear.

"Brother, that man sang to you. *Sang.* Talk about romance. What more could you want?"

Everything. Every boring, mundane, ordinary and wonderful thing. Which doesn't sound like me at all. "You're right."

"I always am. Unless she is."

Austen laughs. "That was exactly the right answer."

I'm not jealous of that perfect-couple banter. At all.

Royal catches my eye as if to say, *See what I mean?*

"Come on, big man," she says, sliding her carryon over her shoulder. "We're about to start boarding."

"Oh, I know. I managed to snag us a few of the best seats, too."

She gazes up at him with interest. "Oh yeah?"

"They might turn into a bed. I'm just saying."

I take a step back and laugh. "I'll say goodbye now before I hear too much."

Royal looks between us, then bends down to give her a kiss. "I'll be right there, Austen."

He hangs back to give me another back-cracking hug. "Wish me luck."

"Why?" I ask. "You've already got the girl. And she'll be trapped on a plane with you for hours."

He pulls back and glances over his shoulder. "If this weekend goes the way I think it will, she'll be trapped with me for a hell of a lot longer." His smile is a beautiful thing. "I love her. And you love Miller, right? Here's to retiring from the pirate's life."

I do love Miller. I have from the first. It just took me a while to figure it all out.

And he loves you, even if he hasn't told you to your face yet. Didn't you listen to the song?

"Have fun, Royal. And good luck."

He nods, grabbing his bag to heft it over his shoulder. "Thanks for keeping our flight schedule to yourself, by the way. Can you imagine the circus if we had her family and mine seeing us off?" He laughs. "If JD knew about it, he'd have flown them all out just to tick me off."

"Luckily, he doesn't have clearance to get all the way to the gate like some of us."

"Enjoy it while you can," Royal teases.

"I will. Now run." I push his shoulder, pretending to panic. "Because if anybody can talk their way around security, it's your brother."

I watch them hand their tickets to the flight attendant and disappear before I turn on my heel and race for the parking garage.

It's time for me to go home.

***

"Oh. My head."

I smile and share a look with Fred. "It lives."

She laughs, grabbing a slice of bacon before heading toward the door. "That's my hint to disappear for a while. I'll be right next door if you need me. Heather promised to help me write some letters to our congressman."

Of course she did. Heather was so proud of Fred for being clever enough to send that video that she would have agreed to anything.

I like Heather.

Diane is…growing on me.

"I'm dying," Miller groans loudly from the couch. "This is why I don't drink."

I step into the living room, a glass of juice and some Advil in my hand. "I don't think you're dying, but I honestly can't be sure. I can't say I've ever had wine from a box before."

Miller goes so still, I wondered for a second if he's fallen back to sleep.

"You're here?" he asks, his eyes still tightly closed.

I sit down on the coffee table across from the couch. "Where the hell else would I be, Millie?"

He looks at me now, his golden eyes uncertain. "I thought you were—"

"I wasn't. I was seeing Royal and Austen off." I lift the glass. "Sit up and drink this for me."

He obeys gingerly, holding his head as if it might dislodge itself. "The dog tripped me, otherwise I would have shown up at the airport and done something seriously embarrassing."

"Like what?" I ask innocently as he takes the pills with his juice.

Miller laughs and then winces at the noise. "I'll never tell. And if my friends ever want to set foot in this house again, neither will they."

"I'm not leaving you," I say, taking the glass from his hand before he drops it.

"You mean today?" he asks uncertainly.

"I mean I'm not leaving you. Period. If I go somewhere from now on, you're coming with me. That's the only way this is going to work."

Miller shakes his head. "I can't fly away every time you do. I have to work. I have Fred. Well, I hope I have Fred. That's not official yet."

I shrug. "And thanks to my father being a rich asshole, I now have more money than either of us could spend in a lifetime. I'm looking into getting my own plane. Might make vacations more fun. And we could bring the dog. What do you think?"

Miller leans back on the couch. "First, I think I need to get a new couch—this one sucks and my neck is hurting."

I feel a sympathetic twinge. "What else?"

"I think I'm still asleep. You can't quit your job. You love your job. You love traveling. You even love your uniform."

"I love *you*," I correct him quietly. "And you happen to be worth sticking around for and making a home with. The job wasn't what I loved, anyway. Just the flying.

Though I do think I looked pretty good in that uniform."

"You do."

"I can wear it for you later." I waggle my eyebrows and he laugh-winces again. "Come on. Let's get you in the shower and then you can eat my delicious, mostly cold bacon."

"Brendan." He stops me at the foot of the stairs and lays his hands on my shoulders. "I need to tell you something."

"I know."

"No, you don't."

"Trust me, Miller."

He glares at me. "You don't know what I'm going to say."

I lean forward, stopping with my lips pressed against his temple. "The first time," I croon, humming a few bars.

He elbows me in the stomach and then stomps up the stairs. "Oh my God, I hate everyone."

"You love me," I call up to him in a teasing sing-song, before following in his wake. "You know you do."

And here I thought I finally had a handle on romance.

6 months later

"Fred is not going to learn to fly before she learns to drive."

I slap Miller's ass as I pass him on the tarmac, making Fred laugh. "Fred's known how to drive since she was thirteen. She just hasn't had a license."

"That's true." Fred untangles Dix from his leash before joining us beside the plane.

My plane.

"I want to fly, Miller," she tells him. "Think of the possibilities. Skywriting, banners…"

I wink at my new husband. "Think of it, Millie. Just think of it."

"Believe me, I'm thinking things," he grumbles.

That feeling when you finally convince your best friend to marry you in a cheesy double ceremony with a big bear of a Samoan and the woman of his dreams? Yeah, I'm finally there.

To say the reception was crowded would be an understatement. The Wayne family, Royal's family—and yes, I'm talking all nine brothers plus one—as well as every member of the Finn clan, since we held it at their pub. It was a lot for Miller to take in, realizing his family was so much bigger than it used to be.

Don't let him fool you, though. He's starting to love the attention.

Austen joked about holding the wedding in an escape room. Thankfully Royal talked her out of it by asking if the marriage would still be legal if they didn't escape in the allotted time.

I even invited Kimmy, the kinky travel agent and my landlord. Plot twist? They're dating. I wanted to thank them for getting me evicted.

It gave me two weeks with Miller Day.

Now I get him for the rest of our lives.

I look at him, wanting to see the expression on his face when he notices the name on the side of the plane. "Do you like it?"

He blinks rapidly before grabbing me by my shirt and pulling me in until I'm close enough to kiss. "I'll show you how much I like it later," he says when he finally lets me go.

"Will you sing it?"

He tries to glare but he can't stop smiling.

"I love you, Millie."

It took a while. But he knows.

…

Oh, the name of the plane?

The Aurelia Day.

It has a nice ring to it, right? We'll be taking her out to an island later this week for our honeymoon.

But today is about family.

"Did Dix just throw up in my plane?"

THANKS FOR READING!

I truly hope you enjoyed this book. If so, please leave a review and tell your friends. Word of mouth and online reviews are immensely helpful to authors and greatly appreciated.

To keep up with all the latest news about my books, release info, exclusive excerpts and more, check out my website **RGAlexander.com**, Friend me on **Facebook**, or follow me on **Twitter**.

If you love the ***Finn Factor*** series and want to hang out with like-minded others, as well as get access to exclusive discussions and enter the frequent ***contests*** and ***free book giveaways*** each month contests, join **The Finn Club** on Facebook:)

Friend me on **Facebook**
https://www.facebook.com/RGAlexander.RachelGrace
to join **THE FINN CLUB**
https://www.facebook.com/groups/911246345597953/
for contests, and smutty fun.

CHECK OUT *Curious*, BOOK 1 OF THE FINN FACTOR SERIES

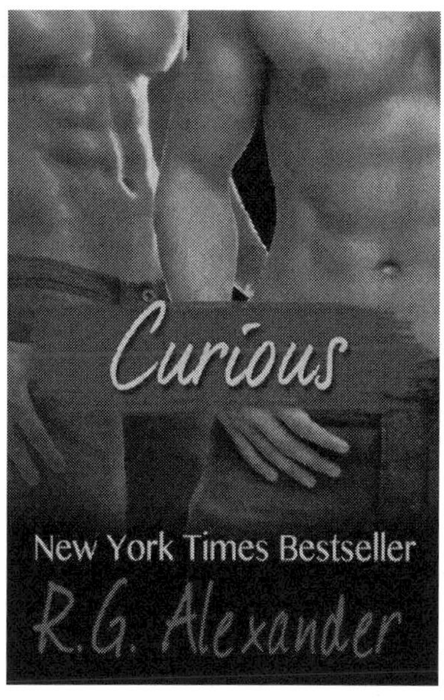

*"Everyone go buy the f***ing thing. Curious. Go now."* tweet
by author of Love Lessons,
Heidi Cullinan

"When I got to the end of this book, I wanted to start over… RG Alexander is one hell of an author!"
USA Today bestselling **Bianca Sommerland**,
author of Iron Cross, the Dartmouth Cobras

Are you Curious?

Jeremy Porter is. Though the bisexual comic book artist has known Owen Finn for most of his life—long enough to know that he is terminally straight—he can't help but imagine what things would be like if he weren't.

Owen is far from vanilla—as a dominant in the local fetish community, he sees as much action as Jeremy does. Lately even more.

Since Jeremy isn't into collars and Owen isn't into men, it seems like his fantasies will remain just that forever…until one night when Owen gets curious.

Warning: **READ THIS!** Contains explicit m/m nookie. A lot of it. Very detailed. Two men getting kinky, talking dirty and doing the horizontal mambo. Are you reading this? Do you see them on the cover? Guy parts will touch. You have been warned.

Available Now!

Check out all the other books in the Finn Factor series.
www.RGAlexander.com

Big Bad John

Bigger in Texas series, Book One

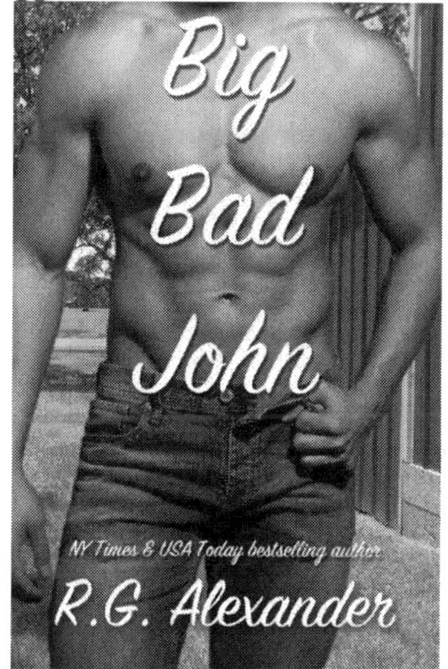

Available Now!

www.RGAlexander.com

Kinda broad at the shoulder and narrow at the hip…

Trudy Adams never planned on going home again. Not to that sleepy little Texas town where everyone knew her business and thought she was trouble. She ran away to California years ago, and now, after what has felt like a lifetime of struggling, her lucky break might finally be around the corner.

And then she got that email.

John Brown has been waiting patiently for Trudy to return, but his patience has run out. He's had years to think about all the things he wants to do to her, and he's willing to use her concern for her brother, her desire to help her best friend get her story, and every kinky fantasy Trudy has to show her who she belongs to.

The explosive chemistry between them is unmistakable. But will history and geography be obstacles they can't overcome? When Trouble makes a two-week deal with Big Bad...anything can happen.

Warning: **READ THIS!** BDSM, explicit sex, voyeurism, accidental voyeurism, voyeurism OF voyeurism with a sprinkle of m/m, exhibitionism, ropes, cuffs, gratuitous spanking, skinny dipping, irresponsible use of pervertables...and a big, dirty man who will melt your heart.

Billionaire Bachelors Series

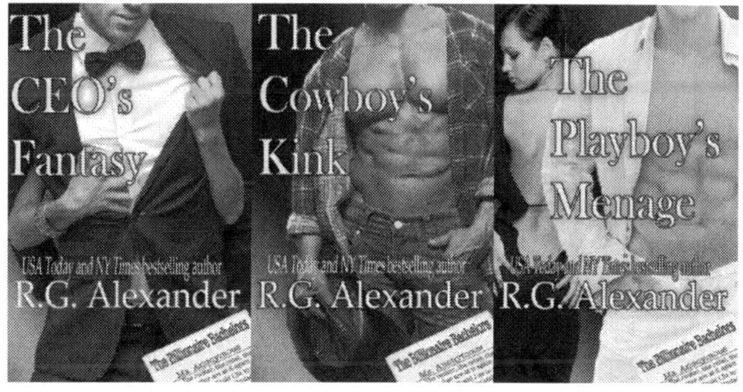

Available Now!
www.RGAlexander.com

Glass slipper shopping can be a dangerous pastime…

The CEO's Fantasy-Book 1

Dean Warren is the billionaire CEO of Warren Industries. He's spent the last five years proving his worth and repairing his family's reputation. But the rules he's had to live by are starting to chafe, especially when it comes to one particular employee. He doesn't believe in coincidence, but when Sara Charles shows up suddenly unemployed and asking him to agree to a month of indulging their most forbidden fantasies--there's no way he can refuse.

When reality is better than his wildest dreams, will the CEO break all of his own rules to keep her?

The Cowboy's Kink-Book 2

Tracy Reyes is a man who enjoys having control. Over his family's billion dollar land and cattle empire, over the women he tops at the club, and over his life. When teacher Alicia Bell drops into his lap with a problem that needs solving and a body that begs to be bound, he can't resist the opportunity to give her the education in kink she needs. But can he walk away from his passionate pupil when it's time to meet his future bride?

The Playboy's Ménage-Book 3

Henry Vincent and Peter Faraday have been friends forever. The royal rocker and polymath playboy have more than a few things in common. They're both billionaires, they both love a challenge...and they've both carried a long-lasting torch for the woman that got away. Finding Holly again brings back feelings and memories neither one of them wanted to face. But they'll have to if they want to share her. Keeping her from running again and making her admit how she feels about them will take teamwork. Hours of teamwork...and handcuffs.

The Bachelors

We know every debutante's mama wants a piece of their action, but if you could choose without repercussions, which of the Billionaire Bachelors would be your fantasy? The true hardcore cowboy who has enough land and employees to start his own country, but no dancing partner for his special kind of two-step? The musician with a royal pedigree, a wild streak and a vast fortune at his disposal, who's never been seen with the same woman twice? His best jet-setting buddy who can claim no less than five estates, four degrees and three charges of lewd public behavior on his record? Or the sweet-talking, picture-perfect tycoon-cum-philanthropist who used to be the baddest of the bunch but put those days behind him when he took over as CEO of his family's company? (Or did he?)

Pick your fantasy lover--rocker, rancher, rebel or reformed rogue. Glass slipper shopping is a dangerous sport to be sure, especially with prey as slippery as these particular animals, but I'll still wish all my readers happy hunting.

From Ms. Anonymous

Available Now!

www.RGAlexander.com

Other Books from R.G. Alexander

Bigger in Texas Series

Big Bad John
Mr. Big Stuff-
Big Trouble-*coming soon*

The Finn Factor Series

Curious
Scandalous
Dangerous
Ravenous
Finn Again
Shameless
Fearless
Lawless
One Wild Finn
Obvious - FREE READ
Relentless

Finn's Pub Romance

One Night at Finn's
Two Weeks and a Day

Billionaire Bachelors Series

The CEO's Fantasy
The Cowboy's Kink
The Playboy's Ménage

Mènage and More

Truly Scrumptious
Three For Me?
Four For Christmas
Dirty Delilah
Marley in Chains

About R.G. Alexander

R.G. Alexander (aka Rachel Grace) is a *New York Times* and *USA Today* Bestselling author who has written over 45 erotic paranormal, contemporary, urban fantasy, sci-fi/fantasy and LGBTQ romance books for multiple e-publishers and Berkley Heat.

She has lived all over the United States, studied archaeology and mythology, been a nurse, a vocalist, and for the last decade a writer who dreams of vampires, airship battles and happy endings for all.

RG feels lucky every day that she gets to share her stories with her readers, and she loves talking to them on Twitter and FB. She is happily married to a man known affectionately as The Cookie—her best friend, research assistant, and the love of her life. Together they battle to tame the wild Rouxgaroux that has taken over their home.

To Contact R. G. Alexander:
www.RGAlexander.com
Facebook:
http://www.facebook.com/RachelGrace.RGAlexander
Twitter: https://twitter.com/RG_Alexander